the Forgotten Black Knights

the Story of Sir Morien and Black Roman London

© 2023
by Aaron Brachfeld
ISBN: 9798872958871

While it would not have been unsurprising to see a black knight in King Arthur's multicultural court, few people today realize that this would be for the same reason there were so many black Roman colonists of Londinium. The noble and antiracist chivalry demonstrated by King Arthur and his knights traces back thousands of years to the most elemental hopes of the Roman people for a more civilized world, and remains relevant even today.

The Story of Sir Morien dates to those dark ages when racism and negrophobia were first encouraged and took hold in Europe. Children and adults alike will enjoy this immensely entertaining and essential chapter of the Arthurian grail cycle and will instantly identify with the young 14 year-old Sir Morien. But they will also find the story to be an inspirational expression of the enduring hope for a post-racist world. As history books are banned across the United States, it has never been so important to learn the reasons for the whitewashing of King Arthur's court and the Roman society upon which it was founded. Black History is Roman History, and also is the Forgotten Black Knights of King Arthur's Court!

Table of Contents

A Black History of the Roman Empire

Rome was an ethnically diverse society. While Roman society did comprehend ethnicity and nationality, it was an essentially colorblind comprehension, lacking our modern concepts of race. So it is challenging to reconstruct the influence and presence of people of color anywhere in the Republic or Empire.

However, though they did not see race, we do. And with our modern color vision we may see them even as they did not see themselves. Sometimes this absence of described color has been used to justify a racist understanding of Rome, and interpreted to express a white and monochrome society. However, the archeological facts yield a much different story.

An archeological survey of human remains in London suggests that as many as 18% of the early settlers of the Roman colony expressed ethnically Black characteristics, and analysis of their bones suggests these colonists were from warmer climates. Further analysis of autosomal DNA suggests that this figure is too low, and the number of black Roman colonists could have been as high as 25%.

But it is unnecessary to reconstruct genetic data when the Romans themselves kept accurate records.

Reading Roman records suggests what was most important to them to notice. The Romans themselves remark most of these first inhabitants of London were involved with the military. But our modern eyes do not see this as the most important characteristic of these men and women. Modern eyes would not see them as soldiers first. Nor as Romans first. We would see them as integral elements of Black History.

And this could be for the better or worse, depending on whether this observation confirmed or refuted our belief in a monochromatic white Roman society.

And this speaks considerably to our own modern world, where it is now important to validate the reality of history against efforts to whitewash it: for it is controversial now to assert that Rome was not monochromatically white.

Let us, therefore, for a moment at least, understand first and foremost they were Roman soldiers. No matter the color of their skin. And in doing so learn from this ancient Empire wisdom for our present day.

To a Roman skin tones did not carry any social implications, and no social identity, either imposed or assumed, was associated with skin color. Although the color black was associated with ill-omens in the ancient Roman religion, these ancients did not fall into the error of biological racism, or believe that people with dark skin had black skin. Further, dark skin color was not a sign of inferiority. Greeks and Romans did not establish color as an obstacle to integration in society. Not as we do today.

Rather, environmental determinism was the primary lens through which classical elites understood their perceived advantage. They strongly believed that certain climates and ecologies developed and influenced culture and human nature, and that some environments were more suited to civilization than others. By changing the land, and cultivating it, we could cultivate ourselves. And it was the obligation of Rome to defend the rudiments of human civilization wherever it might be found - even as a gardener might protect their crop against weeds. So they were ever quick to respond to calls for help: they saw a common enemy of barbarism to all civilized people.

While Romans clearly perceived physical differences between individuals and populations (as evidenced by the frequent representation of diverse types in classical iconography) the thought that there were different races of people would have been utterly foreign to them.

Certainly, the Romans never thought to define these differences in any systematic or comprehensive manner, and terms such as genos, ethnos, ethne and phule can be only approximately mapped onto modern notions of race, ethnic grouping, political units, or other sociocultural concepts. And though the shadow of racism now extends over their tombs, and the lands and legacies they so carefully cultivated, we must remember that the once sun shone brightly on that remarkable society.

This is not to say Rome was without its faults: the concept of human civilization advancing toward a Roman ideal, and other Romanocentricism, is offensive to our modern ideals of a pluralistic society. And today we recognize numerous forms of human civilization, and are slow to declare any entire people barbaric, or savage - even if we do see these traits expressed in people around the world, we might attribute this to human nature, rather than any environmental determinism or cultural weakness.

Nevertheless, a "Roman" identity did not suggest a given skin tone, or even a culture. Rather it referred to an ever-shifting set of legal and philosophical traditions in which inherited physical characteristics were of no relevance whatsoever, and indeed the idea of them bearing any relevance would have been repugnant to the worldview of the Romans - as, perhaps, it should be again to us.

Consider one particularly remarkable account of Africans in England. According to the Augustan History, the Roman emperor Septimus Severus, himself an African, visited Hadrian's Wall in 210 AD. And there he was mocked by other African Romans (from Ethiopia) who were dissatisfied at his governance.

Here the spacious arguments of racists for a monochromatic white Roman society are most tenuous and we may rightly ask:

Was the Emperor not Roman?
Or was he not African?
Or, as some might assert, if African, not a person of color?
Or if a person of color, not truly so, or significantly so, being of mixed racial background? Even though even a drop of such "impure" blood would condemn a man like him to servitude under the racist laws of American slavery, and elsewhere?

Some racists will even go so far as to argue that the fashion of being dark or tanned from exposure to the sun allowed misrepresentations of skin tone in art for men, and the ideals of women being indoors produced misrepresentations of fair skin for them... ***but there is no amount of tanning which can make a white person black,*** nor any duration of avoiding the sun which can make a black person white, nor indeed any amount of light which can make a racist see the historical diversity of European society.

Portrait of the Imperial family of Septimius Severus. Severus, Julia Domna, his wife, and their children – the future emperor Caracalla and Geta. Geta's face was obscured after his murder by Caracalla when Caracalla seized the throne. The graying Severus clearly has dark skin.

We may well ask the same question about other famous African Romans. The second-century rhetorician, philosopher and novelist Apuleius was from Madouros, in what is modern day M'Daourouch, Algeria. Saint Augustine of Hippo studied in the same town. He and Cyprian of Carthage were major figures in Christian theology.

Mauretania is where present day Morocco and Algeria lay, and the provincial term is where the word Moor comes from. Were these men white?

Egypt was a major center of literary and theological innovation in the late imperial period. Are Egyptians white?

A fresco fragment from the Villa of Catullus at Sirmione on Lake Garda. This scholar's ethnicity is clearly understood by modern viewers, but his skin pigmentation would have had less and different meaning to his contemporaries.

In whitewashing European history, especially Roman history, the fallacies of racial theory are laid bare when arguments that Africans like Septimus Serverus were not people of color. Or that West Asian Romans were not people of color - when they are understood to be so today.

The fact that race is an artificial and arbitrary concept needs little explanation. Yet however irrational, it remains relevant: the erasure of Black History from English History, or indeed European History, is one which is as deliberate as much as it is untethered. We must therefore consider its insidious purpose.

There can be little other purpose to whitewashing the ancients other than to convince us that people of color have no historical or modern place in European society, except perhaps as inferiors.

When Aesop himself was Ethiopian, the Medicis find the roots of their family tree in Africa, and noble houses from Russia to England also have African heritage, we must conclude that the mutual influence Africa and Europe had upon each other was profound, and long established.

The question then becomes why therefore seek to deprive Europe of these influences, except to defend a racist ideology that such inferior people were incapable, and owed their capacities to the civilizing influences of Europe? Or is it instead to found argument that they had and have no place in European society except as inferiors?

The Museum of London utilized actors of color to more accurately represent the Roman colonists of London.

Racism has whitened our history. Such whitening was intended toward (and succeeded in) marginalizing and disenfranchising people of color from this heritage. Making Black Romans visible most effectively resists racist mentalities. Therefore, we have an obligation, not only to our modern antiracist sensibilities, but to honor the antiracist philosophies of the ancients, to gaze upon these Black Romans and, by seeing them, affirm the great inheritance of their descendants.

It should not be controversial to say that Black Romans were not unusual, exceptional or few. Nor controversial to assert they were not typically slaves or servants. Black Romans were soldiers and traders, dramatists, poets, philosophers, theologians, knights and Senators, and even Emperors. We need to re-imagine imperial Romans as having a completely unsurprising diversity of skin pigmentation.

We need not even rely on the Imperial records, or archeology. These Romans were proud of their place in the Empire. A stone inscription found in Cumbria shows that in the 3rd century AD a legion of Roman soldiers from North Africa were stationed in Britain. These "Aurelian Moors" were named after Emperor Marcus Aurelius. The word "Moors" tells us that they were from Mauretania – present day Morocco and Algeria.

A Black History of Great Britain

The presence of people of color did not end with the Roman occupation. Yet a continuing colorblindness in those societies that rose after the fall of the Empire again requires our modern color vision to look for them. And they were not typically slaves.

When we do look for them we can see, as clearly as the pigmentation on Septimus Severus's face, a black musician is among the six trumpeters depicted in the royal retinue of Henry VIII in the Westminster Tournament Roll (an illuminated manuscript dating from 1511). He wears the royal livery and is mounted on horseback. The man is "John Blanke, the blacke trumpeter," who is listed in the payment accounts of both Henry VIII and his father, Henry VII.

Part of the 'Westminster Tournament Roll', painted in 1511, John Blanke is in the middle of the row on the right. He was so gifted, the King gave him red clothes, and even doubled his pay (to 16 pence per day) upon Blanke's request.

And similarly, by looking at old pictures, we can clearly see a group of Africans at the court of James IV of Scotland, and can confirm they were also not slaves, but paid wages for their services. A small number of black Africans worked as independent business owners in London in the late 1500s, including the silk weaver who went by the inestimable name "Reasonable Blackman."

To the English of this time, most people of color, if they were described, were described as Moors... even though, strictly speaking, the Moors were a particular and specific nation straddling northwestern Africa and Southwestern Europe, and themselves ethnically diverse.

A Roman soldier, who is Black, is shown embracing a local British woman: this mosaic was found at Low Ham (Somerset), from the Somerset County Museum (Taunton). The portrayal of a typical Roman as having darker pigmentation in his skin is less important to the artist than the message that Britania was being literally embraced by Rome as it became Romanized in culture. Such Romanization by intermarriage was common in many outposts of the Empire and was and remains a method of colonization even today.

This we may confidently say is a fault of geographical knowledge rather than the result of any racism. The phenomenon is similar to how many people today understand "Africans" as including any number of dark-skinned people except, for reasons defying reason or understanding, those people from the lands along its Northern coast...or even how our contemporaries will combine all of "Asia" under one understanding of "Asians" except, for equally mysterious reasons, the Indians, Persians, Arabs, Jews and other West Asians, or even Russians (who are, technically speaking, very much indeed Asian). Geography has always eluded common understanding.

Yet even these "Moors" are whitewashed out of modern awareness.

So where is the line of whiteness drawn? When confronted with this question racists have declared even the Italians are inferior people, and have lynched them in American streets alongside other people of color. But then why are the Romans considered "white" if the Italians are not? Is it due to some mixture of inferior blood?

The reasons for racism are complex, but the resulting whitewashing is predictable. As is the consequence of it: it is because of such whitewashing people of color do not see themselves as integral elements of our own society. The Romans are white because of their influence on so-called Western civilization.

...And so it can come as a surprise to people of color just how very many knights of color there were in King Arthur's Court.

A Black History of King Arthur's Court

In stories knights of color in King Arthur's court are not characterized nor caricaturized; they are written as any white character might be. Nor are they there to merely add "color" to the stories as minor characters: their tales stand alone and as well as any about the many English, French, Dutch, Italian, German or other knights in Arthur's court.

Arthur's court was an international one, one where all people were welcomed by open doors. The diversity of his court was not seen as a strength or weakness by those who wrote about it, for such concepts of diversity would not be developed for hundreds of years. Rather, such diversity was seen as a necessary byproduct of his seeking for the world's noblest warriors to join him: while Arthur's was very much a classist society, and had many faults, it was not a racist one.

Sir Morien as an older man, from an illuminated manuscript circa 1350s, image from Medieval People of Color. However, the story in this book portrays Sir Morien's first adventure as a 14 year old teenager, before he even learned chivalry.

Indeed, in the stories, there was even respect shown to Muslims and other non-Christians; even if there is a strong bias toward the superiority and correctness of Christianity, the nobility of non-Christians is observed, and praised, and frequently the understanding of a shared monotheism serves as a means to develop friendship between those cultures. Even as the villainy of Christians founds the antagonism Arthur's knights must confront if they will continue the noble work of the Romans in civilizing the world's barbarians.

Arthur's court was also not a nationalist one. King Arthur saw one single human expression of nobility, and strength. And, on some rare occasions, even acknowledged that commoners were capable of advancing themselves, ennobling them as well.

The Chivalry of Antiracism

In our series on Black History we have explored many biographies and histories from around the world, and while we have profiled famous authors, but this will be the first time we shall more closely examine a fictional person.

In doing so, we hope you will notice the impossibility of seeing him in the same color blindness of his contemporary audience.

And we should remark now that it is a difficult thing for us to imagine a colorblind society today. One which is still cognizant of different cultures, and nationalities, but which is oblivious to race. Indeed, the recent emergence of an ethnic identity among African Americans in the late 19th Century (already explored in this series) suggests that there is frequently an importance to such an understanding.

King Arthur was always quick to forgive someone if they demonstrated penitence and humility, never confusing punishment for justice. And we must wonder what might become if we hold ourselves to this same noble ideal when exploring European Black History.

It would a long time between noble Arthur and the more narrow minded colonialism of Elizabeth I, who was "highly discontented" at the great number of "Negroes and blackamoors" in her realm - a sentiment shared by the Mayor of London who, in 1731 prohibited people of color from becoming apprentices. And it was a longer time still between Elizabeth I and Elizabeth II, who so far reversed the slaving and colonial policies of her namesake and predecessors as to encourage the independence of the commonwealth nations, returning full circle to the high ideals of Arthur.

But we must see, as Arthur did, a return is possible. And no story of Black History is complete without telling this part of it as well. For there will come a time when these knights of color are once more welcome at the Round Table.

Caroline Watts was the illustrator for one of the first English translations of Sir Morien (1901), and here chooses an unknown white knight for the cover art. In illustrating Sir Morien among the sailors (the caption reads "They deemed they had seen the Foul Fiend himself"), she portrays him as white.

Perhaps it is by returning to ancient literature that we may also return somewhat to their ancient ideals, and find guidance in the wisdom in those supposedly dark and primitive ages. But we should not covet their blindness, for in blinding ourselves will not remove the hatred from our own hearts any more than returning to the dark of night removes the obstacles in our path we see in the morning light.

Rather, it is when we can see all the colors we can better appreciate the dawn - and the bright day to come. It is by seeing clearly we are best prepared for those obstacles in our journey. Seeing every color, we can celebrate every one!

Sir Morien (also spelled Moriaan) was, as his name suggests, a Moor. He was the son of Agloval, one of King Arthur's Knights of the Round Table. His adventures are concentrated in a 13th-century Arthurian romance written in Middle Dutch, a 4,720-line version of which is preserved in the vast Lancelot Compilation, and a shorter fragment at the Royal Library at Brussels. However, he appears as a supporting character in many other tales.

For example, at times, Lancelot disguised himself as other knights. Sometimes this was so he might find battles to test himself, as few knights would give him the opportunity for battle knowing just how strong he was. So, if he appeared as a weaker knight, he might have that chance to better prove himself - and if he remained undiscovered during the battle, bolster the reputation of his weaker friends. But at times, Lancelot disguised himself to avoid discovery while on secret or illicit adventures. Especially those involving

Guenivier. Sir Lancelot would frequently disguise himself as Morien when he wished to both go incognito and not be attacked on the road, so strong was Morien's reputation.

When the BBC portrayed black Romans living in early London in their animated series "the Story of Britain" (the "Life in Roman Britain" episode), there was an objection made that they were "Blackwashing" English history. When the esteemed Roman historian Mary Beard defended the BBC as portraying a historically accurate image of the ethnically diverse Roman Britain, a "torrent of aggressive insults" on social media resulted.

Because this particular story is set in the same storyline of Chretien de Troyes's *Perceval* but written long afterwards, it attempts to synchronize various existing stories about Sir Morien. But it also tries to express that hope for brotherhood and love the Grail stories did: a global world, in which Moors had a part as much as Frenchmen, Englishmen, and others you might see at King Arthur's court.

So how many people of color would you see at King Arthur's court?

Some conservative estimates make 6% of the Knights of the Round Table in the older traditional stories to be ethnically black. Of course, not all the knights of color were black: many were Arabs, Moors, or even Asian. And one of them was even Green. But this is fiction and while we won't see many Green knights today, 20% of today's new knights in Britain are people of color.

For context, to date, only about 1% of Senators in America have been black, about 24 total. 20 of whom served in the 21st Century.

Sir Morien is a popular hero for players in the mobile app game King's Throne. His depiction here is different from ancient literature: notice he is wearing a red cape, rather than entirely black.

Knights of color have never been unusual, even if Senators of color still are. So why did this story suggest that some peasants and nobles might have never seen someone who is black? Or even heard of someone who has dark skin? Why show these peasants displaying negrophobia?

Consider that in other stories, the complexion of Sir Bors was described merely as "dark," and other knights of color are usually described with similarly muted description - because their race did not matter, in any societal or literary way. Indeed, with some knights of color, like the brothers Sir Palamedes, Sir Safir and Sir Segwarides, the fact that they were not Christian mattered much more.

Obviously, in the story of Sir Morien the color of his skin mattered greatly. And we see the author went further, and portrayed Sir Morien's heraldic color as black as his skin.

Some knights, like the (very) black Morien, or the Green Knight (who famously became father in law to Sir Gawain and now has his own major motion picture), or even Sir Feirefiz, Sir Percival's half brother, who was piebald (and compared to a magpie in his appearance and behavior) have the color of their skin (as well as that of their heraldry) emphasized as an essential element of their literary character for symbolic purposes.

Color did have a symbolic meaning, but not the one Americans might recognize. Black represented a concept of monastic virtue, royal luxury, and sincerity.

In heraldry, black is better referred to by the color name "sable." Sable can be traced back to Middle English, Anglo-French, and ultimately to the Middle Low German sabel, which refers to a species of marten known as a sable. This is related to the Middle High German zobel, which is of Slav origin and akin to the Russian sobol, which likewise refers to the sable. Since at least the 14th century, sable has been used as a synonym for the color black. Both sable and negro are used to describe black in Spanish heraldry. In Portugal, black is known as negro, and in Germany the colour is called schwarz.

Whatever they are called, the different colors are traditionally associated with particular heavenly bodies, precious stones, virtues, and flowers, although these associations have been mostly disregarded by modern heraldists.

Sable is associated with the diamond, saturn, prudence and constancy, and nightshade (a balm against many evils).

But it is also associated with bears. And astute readers will notice bears torment Sir Agloval in his vision for his sins, especially for breaking his vow to Sir Morien's mother.

Black is also seen as a beginning color, associated with knights who have not yet begun service to a King, or accepted the codes of chivalry - which also describes Sir Morien exactly.

Here it is easy to see that the color of Sir Morien's heraldry is the essential element of the story, not his skin color. But, to the extent that his skin color emphasizes the heraldry, the Moorish element becomes important.

When Sir Yvain goes mad and appears like a Moor, it is because his "black bile" (believed by contemporary medicine to be responsible for insanity and necrosis) was dominant and had blackened him. He was not insane or wild *like* a Moor, nor were Moors filled with black bile, but Sir Yvain was filled with black bile to the point of *being* dark.

Yet we are still confronted with the negrophobia of the peasants. This is met by an angry response from their nobles. The antiracist response by the nobles to this negrophobia may therefore be inferred to serve as a teachable moment for the audience. Just as Sir Morien did not hesitate to rescue Sir Gawain, his brothers in knighthood do not hesitate to defend Sir Morien from racism or its effects, and gladly force the peasants to serve him as they would any other knight.

From Paul Hector Maire's: De arte athletica, a 16th Century fencing manuscript: fencers are portrayed regardless of race

Though set in England, this story is actually central European in origin. And there are over 1 million Black people in Central Europe today. Most Europeans still don't know of the long history of the Black Diaspora in their countries. As a result, there is a general assumption that Black people are a relatively new presence on the continent and thus are historical and national outsiders.

Such misperception was developed and encouraged during the crusades, when Xenophobia combined with antisemitism and islamophobia to characterize dark skinned people as "others" and "enemies." It was at this time we first see the wider description of devils being blackened by hellfire, or Muslims as devilish opponents of Christianity.

The negrophobia of the peasants in this story is of that sort, for it was written at the time such negrophobia was being institutionally taught. And this suggests the author intended his story of Sir Morien as a poignant counterpoint. What better argument against the racism which is so unChristian, so unRoman, so unEuropean than to tell the story of the blackest of King Arthur's knights?

The baker Terentius Neo and his wife, from Pompeii.

The reader notices readily an inability of peasants to think or be reasoned with in their negrophobia. Or even to observe Sir Morien as being a man. Against this insensibility, Sir Garlet is required to use force to secure their good behavior, and in doing so fulfills his own societal role as a knight and obligations to the Chivalric code.

This story was written in a time of emerging racial awareness, and in those first steps out of the colorblind Roman era to our modern racism we see the same resistance to racism which resonates today.

And hopefully, it is encouraging that there was, since the dawn of this necrophobic racism, an antiracist argument made against that uneducated peasant mentality.

Yet we should also be aware that in hundreds of years such noble arguments have been useless. And it is worth considering that like Sir Garlet, our own modern day "knights" in Little Rock were required to use force when they opened the doors of public schools to that city's children of color. Or how frequently we rely on the magisterial force of our courts to require racists to desegregate bathrooms, restaurants, and presently, to ensure the equal rights of all Americans to vote, or even to receive equal medical care and other basic needs.

Negrophobia is ancient. However, there is hope that even if we never shall again be united under a Roman Emperor, and there is little reason to expect our world will be united in Christian brotherly love any time soon, we may nevertheless see each other as brothers and sisters, and fellow citizens of the same shared world if we ourselves adopt such codes of chivalry and examples of nobility as are presented in stories like Sir Morien's. Perhaps we may, as Arthur did, see that strength and nobility are human virtues, and are far more important than nation, race or religion.

The Tale of Sir Morien begins with a penitent knight's healing and forgiveness. what better way for us to set off upon our own quest, even as Sir Morien did, to find what happened to our fathers? Understanding the rich, diverse heritage we inherit, I have no doubt that we shall all take pride in our own nobility and strength as we find ourselves motivated by their chivalrous examples to unhesitantly and boldly do what must be done today (as true knights ought to) for a more equitable, just, free and noble society!

A Brief History of the Word, "Moor"

The etymology of the word "Moor" is uncertain, although it can be traced back to the Phoenician term Mahurin, meaning "Westerners." From Mahurin, the ancient Greeks derived Mauro, from which Latin derives Mauri.

During the classical period, the Romans interacted with, and later conquered, parts of Mauretania, a state that covered modern northern Morocco, western Algeria, and the Spanish cities Ceuta and Melilla. The Berber tribes of the region were noted in the Classics as Mauri, which was subsequently rendered as "Moors" in English and in related variations in other European languages.

During the Latin Middle Ages, Mauri was used to refer to Berbers and Arabs in the coastal regions of Northwest Africa. The 16th century scholar Leo Africanus (c. 1494-1554) identified the Moors (Mauri) as the native Berber inhabitants of the former Roman Africa Province (Roman Africans).

After the fall of the Roman Empire, the term Moor began to develop new meaning as it became associated with the Muslim religion of Islam that had been widely adopted in the region, and later with a darker skin pigmentation, and later still with anything dark (even being used to describe wines that were dark). As an understanding of racial identity emerged, because the word had been applied to describe darker colors, it was naturally extended to describe people with darker skin pigmentations.

During the conquest of Iberia by the Berber Moors, as well as during the reconquest of Iberia by the Christians, and later the crusades, speakers of Romantic languages, who were by now largely Christian, warred with Muslim peoples. It was at this time the term gained negative connotations, and also developed an understanding of describing an outsider to society, and was even used to describe all muslims, regardless of their ethnicity, race, or nationality.

This said, the Moorish influence on northern African culture, Sicylian culture, and even Mediterranean culture generally was considerable and such generalizations may not have been entirely gratuitous. And with that must come further remark that complex politics combined many ethnic and cultural groups into a single understanding of "Moorish" at the time, even if they were not, in any sense or meaning, from the coastal regions of Northwest Africa.

Of course, the word "Moor" is polysemous, and can also be used to describe a kind of uncultivated heath typical of Northern Britain, the method by which a boat is attached by a rope or anchor to the shore, or various other things, but it is certain these polysemous

words, though they sound similar, and are spelled identically, are
entirely unrelated.

The Tale of Sir Morien

The Penitent Knight

This is the story of the knight named Morien. Some sources suggest he was Perceval's son, while others claim he was the son of Agloval, who was Perceval's brother, making Morien Perceval's nephew. However, it's well known that both Perceval and Galahad died as virgin knights in pursuit of the Holy Grail and so because of this, I believe that Perceval was not Morien's father but rather his brother's son.

Morien was born to a Moorish princess when Agloval was searching for the lost Lancelot.

At the time our story begins, some 14 years after Morien was born, King Arthur ruled in Britain and held a grand party to enhance his reputation as a prosperous and powerful King and make him even more famous. But while the nobility feasted, a wounded knight arrived.

You see, in King Arthur's time, the Court's doors were open to anyone, and everyone could come and go as they pleased. The knight attempted to dismount but was so badly wounded that he couldn't. He was in a dire state, with wounds which seemed likely to be fatal. He arrived looking disheveled, with his weapons, clothing, and his impressive horse all stained red with his own blood. Despite his pain, he managed to greet the lords in the hall as best as he could but couldn't say much due to his injuries.

Then my lord, Sir Gawain, known for his kindness throughout his life, didn't hesitate. As soon as he saw the wounded knight, he quickly got up, helped the knight off his horse, and placed him on the ground. However, the knight was in such bad shape that he couldn't sit, stand, or even stay on his feet; he collapsed onto the ground.

Sir Gawain then instructed them to carry the knight gently onto a couch on the side of the hall, where the important guests could hear his story.

Since the knight could hardly speak, they removed his armor and clothing, wrapped him in warm blankets, and gave him a piece of bread soaked in clear wine.

Then Sir Gawain, known as a skilled healer in those days, examined the knight's wounds. People believed that there was no one better at treating injuries than Sir Gawain. If he took charge of a wounded person, they were almost certain to recover from their wounds!

The knight lying there spoke, "I'm in distress; I can't eat or drink. I feel my strength fading, and it seems likely I will now die. But if I'm granted a chance to speak to the king, whom I sought desperately and came here to avoid breaking an oath, I might find a way to live."

Sir Gawain kindly assured the knight, "I don't think you need to fear death now, for I am here to help, and you will be alright." He took a root from his pouch that had the power to stop bleeding and restore strength. He placed it in the knight's mouth and encouraged him to eat a little. This eased the knight's suffering considerably, and soon he even began to eat and drink, even forgetting his pain.

After the knight was thus recovered, King Arthur approached the wounded knight and greeted him, "God give you a good day, dear Sir Knight. Please, tell me who wounded you so severely and how you got hurt? Did the knight who harmed you escape without injury?"

The knight spoke to the king, "I will tell you the truth because I am bound by my oath. It was seven years ago when I lost all my possessions, and I fell into such poverty that I didn't know what to do. I turned to robbery to survive. I had already sold my tithes, spent all my wealth, and mortgaged my home and lands. I had nothing left of what my father had left me when he passed away. I was completely impoverished. However, I had become impoverished by being generous, giving away my wealth to whoever would ask it, whoever was in need I helped without hesitation. I never turned away anyone seeking assistance, whether they were squires, pages or messengers or anyone else, and I always made sure they received something."

The knight continued, "but with nothing to support me, and homeless, I did many evil things. Initially, I felt ashamed, but if I encountered people, whether they were pilgrims or merchants carrying goods and money, I used various means to take it for myself. Having once given away everything, now little escaped my grasp."

The King listened patiently as the knight continued. "Three days ago, as I was on my way, I came across a knight, and I admired his horse so much that I desired it more than anything I ever had. When I tried to take the reins and told him to dismount, he immediately drew his sword and struck me with such force that when I regained consciousness I had forgotten who I was and everything that happened to me. Coming to, I saw he was continuing to attack, and I became aware of my situation. I then tried to defend myself, but his blows were so fierce, they pierced through my armor as if I wasn't even wearing any, cutting flesh and bone. And though I was armed, I couldn't land a single blow on him that could harm him! So, I had to surrender and promised, if I wanted to save my life, to come here to you as quickly as possible and not delay, and face your justice. I now fulfill that promise by presenting myself to you, Sir King, and confessing my wrongdoings in this world, for I regret them all."

The King then asked, "do you know who sent you here? What was the name of the knight?"

The knight did not know.

So the King asked, "can you describe his horse and any distinctive signs?"

The knight replied, "I can't tell you much, except that the knight's horse and armor were as red as blood. His accent was Welsh. He's incredibly powerful, and I doubt you'd find his match in all of Christendom. I can honestly say I wish I had not encountered him when I had such bad intentions."

King Arthur then exclaimed, "oh! That would be Sir Percival!" King Arthur explained to the knight Sir Percival had helped many other evildoers regret their misbehavior while seeking for the Holy Grail, and had not returned to Court in a long time. And wouldn't return until he succeeded in his quest. But he was unlikely to succeed, and the King was grieved to be without Sir Percival's help and company for so long - for they were good friends. Everyone was sad and quiet to hear the King so sorrowful.

Sir Kay then offered to bring Sir Percival back, whether he was willing or not. At this King Arthur and the rest of the Court smiled again and even laughed. "Sir Kay, you don't seem to remember the last time you offered to bring Sir Percival back against his will! You broke your collarbone when you landed feet upwards after being knocked off your horse!"

Sir Gawain then said, "you remind me of an old saying, Sir Kay: how, if some men grow old, and God should spare them even to live 100 years, then they would never grow any wiser, but become even more foolish. Now, listen to me, you once did find Sir Percival, and said to him what he would not hear. I know Sir Percival well, and when he is treated with respect he is gentle as a lamb, he is courteous to all the world, rich and poor, so long as men do him no wrong. But you seem to rouse him to such anger that he becomes the fiercest wight of God's making. By the Lord above, you are not the man to do this, and if you tried you would put yourself and our King to shame."

So spoke Sir Lancelot, and all those gathered in the hall.

Gawain then said, "But by the might of our Lord who rules in Heaven, and in his name, I will find Perceval and, if he doesn't mind coming with me, bring him to Court, and will not rest in one place more than a night or two until I have found him."

King Arthur then said "God knows this brings me joy and sorrow. For I would like to see Perceval again, but I cannot spare you. Yet, nephew, I would not have you break your oath, therefore make ready as you see fit and depart swiftly, and find Perceval."

With this Sir Lancelot of the Lake stepped forward and spoke, saying he would adventure himself and take what fortune would send him, and seek Perceval through all the lands. "Because the King will be freed from care if he can have Perceval, I will now ride for his honor. And if I should find that knight, if it is in my power, I will bring him here. So now I will also make myself ready, and ride forth without any delay.

Arthur said, "Sir Lancelot, it may behoove you to think better of this. It may turn to my shame if all my knights rode forth, and thereafter I was beset with war - as it has happened in the past. So it might be my undoing, for I would have in the past lost my crown and lands but for my knights and only by them have I been victorious."

But Lancelot would not be left behind: "by the Lord who made me, and who will be our Judge on the last day, come whatever may from my choice, if Sir Gawain rides I will not be left behind. Rather, I will try what may chance, and adventure all that God gave me. For, you remember, once he once sought me with all his power and rescued me when I needed him to, and brought me once more to court - and for that I owe him my faith and fellowship."

So Sir Gawain, who did not forget the wounded knight and his need of healing, went to him where he lay and bound his wounds and so tended him that he was quickly healed. And then all the Court was sad at the departing of Sir Gawain and Sir Lancelot, that they ate but little.

But now we will be silent on their lamentations, and henceforth tell of Sir Gawain and Sir Lancelot when they rode on their way.

The Black Knight

In the morning, as soon as it was day, Sir Gawain and Sir Lancelot rode together through the wilderness, over heath and hill, through many valleys to seek Sir Perceval. But they could learn no clue as to where he might be, and so they were growing frustrated.

On the 9th day, there came riding toward them a knight on a good horse, and well armed. His shield and his armor were Moorish, and black as a raven. His head, and his hands were all black. His entire body was black - except his teeth, which he smiled at them. He rode his horse at a full gallop, and drew near to the knights, and after they had exchanged friendly greetings, he said to Sir Lancelot, "now, knight, tell me what I want to know, or guard against my spear! I will know the truth to my questions, and you will answer me or I will fight you! And answer quickly, or you may regret it!"

Sir Lancelot replied, "I would rather die than live as a shamed knight who is forced to do what he doesn't want to do. Fight me if you like, but I am more inclined to fight you than not - if only to diminish your pride and chastise your discourtesy, even if I must die for it."

This made the Moor angry, and so he reined back his horse, and laid his spear in the rest, keen to fight. Without a word, Sir Gawain drew off to one side. Though Sir Gawain would have wanted to help Sir Lancelot, it would have been discourteous for the two knights to fight one. Besides, he was near enough to help Sir Lancelot if he fell into trouble. So he stood still and silent, as one not inclined to fight or break the laws of courtesy. Now he saw better that this knight was even taller than Sir Lancelot, and his horse was bigger, too.

The two knights rushed together, Sir Lancelot and the Moor, and each broke their spears as if they were reeds! Yet neither fell from their horses. So each then drew their swords from their sheathes, and set to work upon each other. God must have willed that they would live, for if any of their strokes had landed, neither man would have escaped alive. Even in the broad daylight, the sparks that flew from helmets and swords could be seen clearly falling upon the flowers and grass at their feet. Certainly, the smiths that wrought their weapons and armor made them perfectly, and merited a greater reward than even any King Arthur ever gave for such work.

Neither the Moor nor Sir Lancelot would yield until Sir Gawain interposed himself between them and parted them by a prayer, and made them withdraw from each other. He said it would be a great pity for either or both of them to die. He said to the Moor, "this is a bad habit you are in, and you will henceforth renounce it. Had you but only asked us courteously what you wanted to know this knight would have answered it out of his good will," then speaking to Sir Lancelot, "and you! You are both rash and foolish. And you will both lose by it."

The Moor took objection. "How dare you speak this way to me! Do you not know I am unafraid to fight against the both of you together? Even if you were Sir Gawain and Sir Lancelot, who are the finest knights alive, I wouldn't yield a foot to you!"

Sir Gawain thought to himself, "we have indeed been foolish to fail to show courtesy to one who praises us so highly!"

But hearing this Sir Lancelot had then an even greater desire to fight or play it to a loss. So Sir Gawain, who knew Lancelot well enough to know this, prayed Sir Lancelot, by the love they shared, and for the sake of King Arthur, that for their honor he should hold his peace a while and let the Moor say his will. Still, Sir Lancelot would fight the Moor. So Sir Gawain then asked him to hold his peace for the faith he owed to Guenevere, his uncle's wife.

At this Sir Lancelot spoke, "truthfully, if you had not just now charged me so I would have avenged myself or been slain. This knight has forced strife upon me without cause, and loaded me with blows. But you remind me, I would be a man who will harm no other unless he attacks me first. I will be at peace, but I do it not out of cowardice, but for love." He paused, thinking better of what he was to say. "For love of you, and your prayer."

So the three stood there, and Sir Gawain addressed the Moor, saying "you are truly foolish: since neither of us nor you are truly harmed, we can now do lightly that which would have otherwise cost you your life. Tell me what you want to know, what you should have asked respectfully of this knight, and I will answer you."

The Moor, calmer, acknowledged Gawain was right. "Do you know anything about Sir Agloval, the brother of Sir Perceval of Wales? I have asked many this question, ridden here and there for 6 months, daring many perils, and now you will tell me, in friendship or fight, if you know anything of Sir Agloval. We have had enough of talk, it is for you to answer, or we will take up our strife again, and see which of us sooner takes his fill of it."

Gawain smiled at the Black Knight, "first you tell me what you know of Sir Agloval, and why you seek him, and then I will tell you everything I know."

So the Moor answered straight away: Sir Agloval is my father. When he came to the land of the Moors, through his valiant deeds he won the heart of a maiden, my mother. The matter went further, by their words and courtesy, and because he was so handsome and she so beautiful, each pledged their vows to each other, and she gave him all he wanted. And this brought her small reward and great sorrow. For he forsook her thereafter."

The Black Knight shook his head. "It's been 14 years, and when he parted from her she bore me, though he did not know she was pregnant. He told her his quest, and the reason he had to leave her: he was seeking a noble knight, lost at the time, Sir Lancelot. Apparently, according to my mother, he and many of his fellows had sworn a great oath to seek Sir Lancelot, and though they looked for him for two years, they could not find him or learn anything of him. They had sworn to not stay in one place more than a day or two, and for this reason, my father could not break his oath, but had to leave my mother. But before he departed, he swore to her that he would return when he achieved his quest. But he has not kept his oath. Therefore, I sought him. If he is alive, I pray to God he is ashamed of himself, but if he is already dead, I pray God forgive him for his sins."

The Knight continued, "My mother and I are by his shame disinherited, since he deserted us, and I was greatly harmed, for they called me fatherless, and I could show nothing against it. So I caused myself to be dubbed a knight, and swore a great oath that I would never meet a knight but I would fight him unless he told me something concerning my father. Even if I would meet my own brother I would not break this oath. And so, if we will part in friendship, tell me what you know and we shall end our conversation. Otherwise, let us end this matter as we began it, for there is no knight under the sun for whom I would break my oath."

At this sad story both Sir Gawain and Sir Lancelot cried. Such pity they had for him, they grew pale, and blushed, when they heard his complaints. Sir Lancelot spoke first. "Nevermore will I be angry for your lack of courtesy. You need no longer stand on guard against me, my heart is not evil toward you, and I will answer you well."

Then the Black Knight drew near to Lancelot and took off his helmet in courtesy, and bared his head and Sir Gawain and Sir Lancelot saw his hair was also black - but they knew Moors are all black, like burnt brands. But do not think this meant the knight wasn't handsome! All men would praise him: what if his skin were black, is that worse than if it were fair? I assure you, in this Moor nothing was unsightly; and besides being handsome, he was taller by half a foot than any other knight - and this when scarcely more than 14 years old!

Now the Moor knelt before Sir Gawain and Sir Lancelot, but Sir Gawain raised him up and told them how they were messengers of

King Arthur, seeking Sir Perceval and Sir Agloval, who was with him. "The King would speak with them, and we are to by any means persuade those noble knights to return straightaway to the King's court and honor his desire. They belong to the Round Table, and have been for a long time. Both are of the King's Court, and are of high renown. Now if you will work wisely, you would go to King Arthur's Court, for I hope Sir Agloval will come there in a short time. Or perhaps you will hear of him - for there tidings come from afar. The King will receive you well there, if you tell him who you are, and the quest upon which you ride. He won't let you depart before we come and bring with us your father, if God prospers us so. Even if you should ride throughout this land, and fight every knight you find, it seems you will need great good fortune to win every battle without mischance. Whoever would always be fighting and never avoid combat will not do so for long. Eventually, you will find your match. Now, Sir Knight, do what we ask, for your own honor's sake, and you will be well at ease there in many ways."

When the Moor heard these words he laughed with his whole heart, smiling, his mouth wide open to show his teeth, white as chalk. "God our Father reward you, noble knights, for the good will and honor you have done me, and also for the great comfort with which you have lightened my heart, which has been too long heavy. If my horse does not fail me I will ride wherever you bid me, to this King you praise so highly."

With that he pledged to the knights hand and knighthood, and called to God to witness that.

Then Sir Lancelot said, "Knight, if you be in any need, when you come into King Arthur's land, I know all will be unknown to you, but speak of us two here to whomever you find and all men will do you nothing but honor and courtesy, wherever you come, in any place. And when you come to the King, before you tell him anything else, say you have seen and spoken with us, and trust me, without fail, you will be well received."

The Moor replied, "it is well said and God reward you for this courtesy! But I cannot say I have seen and spoken with you if I do not know your names."

Then straight away Sir Gawain told him who they were, and how they came to that place, and immediately the Moor fell upon his knees before them. Sir Gawain raised him up, but the Moor laid his hands together and said, "God the Father of all, Ruler of the World, grant that I may amend my misdoing to your honor! Sir Lancelot, my very dear Lord, I own myself right guilty, for I did evil, and nothing else!"

Sir Gawain spoke, "take not to heart what here has chanced, it shall be nothing the worse for you."

Then Sir Gawain and Sir Lancelot mounted upon their horses and prepared to leave. But then the Moor spoke loudly, "no, it is labor lost! Such good knights as you are, since you at this time fare to seek my father, by the power of our Lord I will not stay behind. It would be a shame if I did. I shall ride with you two!"

Sir Gawain replied by making him swear to abide by the ways of chivalry. "If you would ride with us, you must stop being so outrageous as to fight with everyone who you meet. Swear that whoever you will meet on your way, greet tem courteously, and let them pass on their way without fighting, and be their friend if they have done you no wrong. But, if he is fierce to you, or another, only then will you prove your prowess upon him - if only to humble his pride, if you may. And you shall swear to honor all women, and keep them from shame. Be courteous and gentle to everyone you meet who are as well mannered to you, but whoever has no love for virtue, spare them not your sword, spear or shield!"

The Moor agreed. "I will do as you ask since you want it so, may God be gracious to me!"

At the Crossroads

The three rode together until they came to a crossroads where there stood a beautiful cross, on which were written letters red as blood. Sir Gawain, learned in clerkly lore, could read letters. And so he explained to the others what was written, for upon the cross was a warning: "this cross marks the border of Arthur's lands. Any man who comes to the cross is warned to think well upon leaving Arthur's lands, since he can not ride far without strife and conflict, and without finding such adventures that might easily and quickly turn to his harm, or even to his death - for the land beyond Arthur's is of such custom."

Nearby to the cross there was a hermit's retreat. The cabin was well built, and beautiful. While the three knights discussed the warning on the cross, they thought the hermit must have made the cross, and that they might ask the hermit more precisely what danger it was meant to warn against. They thought they might also inquire if the hermit had seen Sir Percival.

Going to the hermitage, they saw the hermit inside, and he seemed to be a good man. They dismounted at his little window and asked the meaning of the cross, and also his tidings: perhaps a knight in red armor had passed this way?

The good hermit answered and said he had seen such a knight, it was just the other day before noon: there were two knights who were remarkably similar to each other. "It seemed to me by their gestures and features they were brothers. Their horses were beyond weary, and they came from the road to Britain. They were both handsome men, and one of them did have a horse and armor red as blood. They dismounted at the foot of the cross you see over there."

While the three knights listened and thought upon this, the hermit told them about the cross. "I have seen many judgments given at that cross: once a knight lost his life, he and his wife with him. They deserve their memory to be held in honor by friends of our Lord, for they made a good ending. They had sought the shrine of a saint, and with them the money and horses, besides other goods - as befits folks of high degrees. Here they were attacked by a company of robbers who slew the good knight, and took his horse and his money, all that he had. Of this his wife was so sorrowful that for grief and woe her heart and spirit broke. Sothey both died here, at the crossroads, where you see that fair cross. The cross was erected as the knight's last wish."

The hermit continued, "Now, folk come here barefoot and naked, doing penance for their sins. And those who pass by mounted on horses or traveling by foot have had many a prayer granted here. The knights of whom you ask stopped to pray, as well befit good knights like them, but I cannot tell you where they went upon their departing for when they left I was saying my own prayers here inside and did not watch them and soon forgot all about them. But they were tall and strong, and one wore red armor, and the other bore the badge of King Arthur."

The three knights were grieved to hear this, since they could not guess which way to go by any craft. So they asked the hermit the manner of the lands where the roads led. "I will tell you as best I may. The road by which you came you already know. And the road which runs straight from there you should avoid, if you heed my advice. It is a land of misfortune, where men follow evil customs. Their best is the worst of other lands. Whoever will keep his horse, weapons and his life will avoid that road. And the right-hand way goes into a wilderness where no men live. I think it is well over a year since I saw ever a man or woman come from there. If you take that road you will find something marvelous and dangerous in your adventure, and may well lose your life or limbs - for there you will find the most dangerous beast anyone has ever heard of. It is the Devil himself, which roams in the shape of an animal. Against him no weapon serves: there was never a spear so sharp nor sword so well tempered that they will not break or be bent without even harming this devil. He lives in a little forest, and there he abides at night, but during the day he prowls by both straight and winding ways. He devours man and animal alike, and I cannot tell you all the horrors I have heard about him. He emptied the entire land there, driving every person away so that now it is a wasteland and wilderness, and none remain. As for the left-hand way, it leads nearby to the sea coast - and there is nothing more remarkable to be said about it."

Lancelot was impatient. "By the Lord who made me, Sir Gawain, there are three of us, and three ways to choose - and we must depart quickly if we will catch up to these knights, for they cannot have ridden far. You ride on whatever road you will, but I will take the way that seems the most dangerous. If you find them, bring them back to this crossroads, and tell the hermit how matters have gone with you that he may tell me if I am able to return here as well. And if this knight goes with you," he gestured at the Moor, "God keep you both, and be a friend to him, do him honor as a good man and true, in whatever place you may go - this much I ask of you."

Sir Gawain answered, "my dear comrade, what you ask sounds good to me. May God protect us in life, limb and worldly honor. Now choose whatever road you will take, for I do not want to wait here any longer."

Sir Lancelot considered the choices carefully. "I think that it is of the most pressing need to fight against the beast against which the hermit has warned us. I think it was well that I rode there."

At this the hermit groaned. "Alas! Oh, Sir Knight, I doubt there are any knights your equal, but you choose an adventure which no man may achieve. All the people have fled out of that land for a reason: none can withstand this beast! This beast shoots venom upon all who go near him more dangerous than any arrow, and whoever this venom lands upon dies within three days - even if he has no wound upon him for it to enter. And it is a far worse way to die than by an arrow. This beast is larger than any horse, and faster. You would be wise to avoid this fiend. If this beast had not chosen to make that place its home, it would have laid the entire world to waste. You would do well to turn back!"

But it was labor lost: not for all the riches of King Arthur would Sir Lancelot have changed his mind.

Now the Moor spoke to Sir Lancelot and Sir Gawain. "What do you take me for? Am I lesser or weaker than either of you that I need Sir Gawain to ride with me? I will not have it so. There is no knight so bold that I cannot withstand him. This is unfitting. Now send me on whatever path you would, I will dare the venture, be it ever so perilous. By my knighthood, and by all who follow Christendom, I shall adventure it alone and take what may chance."

Sir Gawain shook his head. "I don't like this. But since this is your will, take the road to the sea - for this seems to me to be the safest. Ride swiftly and spare not your horse, but seek your father! And if you meet any man, give him a courteous greeting. And then ask him if he has seen your father riding, or otherwise met with two knights, one who wore red armor, the other bearing King Arthur's badge. And if you come to a crossroads, ask men nearby the way to the sea. And if the men you meet do not know the way, return to this place quickly and without delay. Do as I say and I tell you truly, no harm will befall you."

The Moor replied, "God reward you!" Then the three knights took leave of each other, and departed apart.

Sir Gawain at the River

An hour after Lauds at dawn, at the hour of Prime, Gawain had come to a wide and deep river. It was a great stream, and deep, and the current ran swift and strong. This Sir Gawain marked well and took heed when a knight came riding toward him on the far bank.

The knight was on a beautiful horse, and armed for combat. Before him he drove a captive maiden. Sir Gawain saw him strike her again and again, blow upon blow, with a fist that weighed more heavily for the mailed gauntlet that he wore. Though he was clearly causing her considerable pain in this way, he also struck her from time to time with his shield.

The woman wore a robe of green silk, and this was torn in many places - and clearly, this damage had been done by the knight. She rode a sorry looking hack horse, barebacked, and her once beautiful silken yellow hair hung as low as the horse's croup. But now she had lost nearly half of her hair, which fell even as Sir Gawain watched the knight tear it from her scalp.

The scene was past belief, the maiden's sorrow and shame and fear as she wept and wrung her hands: it seemed to Sir Gawain she could not bear another blow.

When Sir Gawain overcame his shock, he deemed it would be his shame would he not avenge this wrong. He looked before and behind him, but saw no bridge by which he might cross the river, nor did he see any ford. He then became aware there was no other living soul about him. He understood he could delay no longer, so he turned his bridle and set his horse toward the river bank and struck his spurs sharply and sprang into the middle of the river.

His good horse bore the current as best it could, turning its breast into the current, swimming as it might, and managed to bring its master to the other side. It was a marvel that neither drowned, for the river was quite deep, and ran very swiftly.

When Sir Gawain climbed the far bank, he was then able to see a great company of folk about a mile off riding hard after the knight. But he did not know for what reason they chased him, whether to aid the knight or to seek their revenge upon him. He saw many of the men in the company were clad in hauberks, and prepared for battle. But his choice was clear and Sir Gawain turned his horse and rode swiftly after the knight to rescue the maiden, intent to avenge the wrongs she had suffered.

As he approached, she saw Sir Gawain and shouted to him, "Noble knight, for the honor or womanhood, save me! This knight does me undeserved shame!"

Such a plight would have stirred any man to pity, and Sir Gawain's heart broke with sorrow and compassion. He called to the knight he was pursuing, "Sir Knight! It is folly and discourtesy that you would do so to this maiden! Were you wise, you would forbear, even if the woman has wronged you, you should deal with her courteously. He has small honor who thus strikes a woman!"

The cruel knight said, "You are a fool and meddler, and whether you are actually a knight or not, I will not stay my hand. No, rather for your shame, I will chastise her the more, and if you but speak another word to her I will knock you off your horse with my spear!"

"Then I would fight you afoot, Sir Knight! Nevertheless, I again counsel you, if you were wise, you would spare the maiden. You will not find me so craven today as to let you harm her again. I will defend her and avenge her wrong, even if my life is risked upon it. But, Sir Knight, listen to my prayer, for God and for your honor, and the sake of knighthood!"

The evil knight said he would in no way do this. "If you will not fly now, by heaven it shall be your Judgment Day. I have no need for your sermons!"

Sir Gawain warned the knight one last time, "Let the maiden go in peace or be on guard against my spear, for I defy you!"

The knight was so high and scornful that Sir Gawain had threatened him that he sought to quell his pride. And so, without any further words, rode against him straight away. Seeing this, Sir Gawain did the same. They came together keenly, both spears broke and the crash was heard afar; the knight was thrust from his saddle and fell to the ground so heavily that he lay in anguish from the fall, prone upon the ground, unable to get up.

Sir Gawain left him laying there, but took the knight's horse and gave it into the hand of the maiden. He then turned again to the knight and drew his sword. At this point, the knight had somewhat recovered, and standing as best he could, drew his sword as well. Evil was his thought, and he cried out to Sir Gawain, "Vassal! How bold you are to do me this hurt and shame! Do not think you shall escape, it is folly what you have done! My father is lord of this land, and after him shall it be mine. Even today you will be repaid by those who follow after me! My men will be here shortly, and you will not escape them, for in this land there is no man who may withstand me!"

"I do believe that," said Gawain. "And that is probably the reason you are so cruel and outrageous. It is a great pity that one of such a noble birth, and wealthy too, should be so false of heart. But I think you are not at such a pass that I might not teach you moderation and humility. I think that today you will regret the evil you have done. I counsel you, if you are wise, that you will tell me how this lady has wronged you. If she indeed deserved such cruelty, then it will be a matter between you two - I will meddle no further. But if the maiden has not deserved this, then hold your hand and make peace with me, otherwise your life is forfeit, no matter how highly you were born, and I shall take the maiden with me when I ride hence."

The knight would not say what the maiden had done to him, so the maiden spoke. "Noble knight, since he will not, I will tell you why he has done this wrong. He would have me for his lover - why should I deny the truth? When he first spoke to me I did not hearken to him - other sorrows vexed me. My poverty grieved me, and I suffered hardships that I cannot lightly tell you of. My father was a knight, and a good man, and of high birth. Dear Sir Knight, I will tell you openly, though it is a shame, that my father had lain sick seven years, and thus lost all his goods, and even now lies in sore straits. He cannot walk, nor stand upon his feet and suffers much pain. Now, I have nursed and tended and otherwise served my father myself - few friends he had except myself, and I had to stay by him and keep him all my life, doing for him all that within me lay in my power. Today this knight came within our hold (which is broken down and ruined) and done me wrong: he took me there by force, and has not stayed his hand from me for God or man. He left his folk behind so that they may hinder my friends, lest they follow him to his hurt. I fear his folk will be here soon, and if they find you here, you will not escape. Save your own life then, Sir Knight, and make a swift end of this combat! I fear it endures overlong and ask you to aid me, by our Lord's grace. So bethink you, Sir Knight, on what you will do."

Sir Gawain spoke to the evil knight, saying "Sir Knight, you will now speak - I will wait here no longer. Will you right this maiden of the wrongs you have done to her, or will you fight me? The one or the other you must now do. And if you like, I will dismount and meet you on foot, or permit you to mount your horse again - upon your promise that you will not use it to flee or escape, but abide your fortune here with me."

The knight answered quickly, "you must think me to be feeble, if you think I would thus yield to you. You will do well to dismount straight away, if you have lust to fight!" He covered himself with his shield, and drew forth his sword from the scabbard. Sir Gawain then dismounted, and let his horse Gringalet stand beside him - never a foot would that horse stir until its lord came and once more laid hand upon it.

Immediately, they betook themselves to fight, an dealt each other fierce thrusts with strong and mighty strokes so that their blood streamed out through the mails of their hauberks, and sparks sprang out when their helmets were smote until they seemed to glow like hot iron when thrust into the furnace, turning red from the fire.

Sir Gawain was distressed that his sword seemed useless against the evil knight's armor, not even scoring the metal. But considering his problem, he instead aimed his sword above the armor at the neck of the evil knight and struck him in the very middle of his throat. Thus the matter was ended: the evil knight's head fell upon his own breast, and the knight fell dead from the blow.

This his friends and kinsmen saw from afar, and it was not long before they came and saw their lord lying dead upon the field. They were stirred to great anger. Seeing their anger grow, Sir Gawain mounted again upon Gringalet, so he might fear them less: his horse was so strong and great! The horse watched everything, ready to follow whatever sign its master might give.

The evil knight's folk were of one mind that they should beset Sir Gawain, behind and in front, on horse and afoot, to kill him. Sir Gawain, seeing he was sore bestead, commended himself to the grace of God with a good heart, and received his enemies with drawn sword. With each blow he killed or wounded one or two, and wrought them such harm they might never find healing for their wounds. It was a good cause for which Sir Gawain fought, and for which he desired vengeance, and this fell to his profit: thus Sir

Gawain, the Father of Adventure, daunted them all so that they drew aside and left the fighting, wounded.

As Sir Gawain was winning, a riding company of the maiden's folk arrived, and they were eager to avenge her shame. She was glad to see them! But when they saw the number and strength of the evil knight's folk attacking Sir Gawain, they left him on the field, daring not to take part with him against their shared enemies - so greatly did they fear them. Instead, they took the maiden from that battle back to her father. But Sir Gawain did not mind. He went on smiting blow after blow on all who came near him, and so drove them back until he was alone upon the field. Those few who survived Sir Gawain that day will tell the story of the battle until Judgement Day!

Now, seeing all his enemies lay dead or wounded, and not knowing where the maiden had been taken to, he could think of no better course of action than to continue his journey he had begun that morning before he saw the maiden. He thanked God he had thus won honor on such evil folk, and that he and his horse had escaped with their lives, free from any mortal wounds, for God had protected them. It is often said, and it is true, that whoever does not think upon his actions but does that which is displeasing alike to God and the world will be unlucky as if they were born in a evil hour - but Sir Gawain was lucky, and won the fight; God had shown him favor by granting him good knighthood and the discomfort of his enemies.

It was now more than 9 hours after sunrise, time for afternoon prayers, and Sir Gawain had neither ate nor drank - nor done anything else except fight that day, and receive great blows. So he rode on his way, perplexed as to where he might find lodging, food and rest. As he rode for hours and the day drew toward evening he saw a castle on a hill. Never was a man more oppressed with hunger, thirst and weariness! And so Sir Gawain thought in his heart that he could do nothing better than to ride there, and see if by chance he might find lodging for the night.

He found by the castle moat the lord of that hill and many of his folk with him. And when he dismounted on the turf he greeted them all courteously, and the lord answered "God reward you!"

Gawain responded, "were it your command, will and pleasure, I would abide here within for the night. I know no other way I might otherwise win shelter. I have ridden all this day, and have found nothing but wilderness and wasteland, and found no one else with whom I might abide the night."

His host said, "so may good befall me in soul and body as I will give you in friendship: even to the uttermost, all that belongs to me. Lodging I will give you, and food - ham and venison. My lodging is ever free, and never refused to any knight who would be my guest. You will have safe conduct, good and sure, against all whom you may meet in this land, even if it were it against my own son, whom I love above all. My safe conduct is so assured that whomsoever wrongs my guest will pay with his life, and all he has. This I swear by my knighthood and the Blessed Maid, Our Lady!"

This being a usual enough assurance (for frequently enough a traveler might come to harm when seeking shelter), Sir Gawain now was reasonably assured of safe shelter for the night and set himself at ease against any mischance. But he did not know that this was the father of the evil knight he had killed in battle earlier that afternoon.

The Capture of Sir Gawain

The host desired to do honor to his guest and took the knight by the hand, leading him into a beautiful golden hall where he was received with courteous words. They disarmed him straight away, and stabled his horse well. Sir Gawain was sat at table, and ate and drank enough that he forgot all sorrow. But then as he was relaxing there, he heard wailing and lamentations, and folk standing outside the walls at the master gate who cried aloud, "alas! alas! let us in!"

Sir Gawain's mood changed instantly, for his heart told him sorrow and mischief were near. He flushed red as his host asked what company stood without and what tidings they bore, and bade them open the gate. The folk without came in, bearing a bier, and making so great a cry and lamentation that men heard it throughout the castle. They came into the hall and cried with a loud voice to the lord of the castle, "alas, master, here lies dead the best knight in the entire world, your dear son! There was no one else on earth so strong, so bold, so skilled in valliant deeds!"

Then all the castle was aghast, and the host, father of the knight who lay dead upon the bier, felt his heart die within him. He could not find words. At last, he cried, "who has robbed him of life, my dear son, whom I loved above all the world? How did he come by his death? I fear it was by his own deed and merited his own death, for I know well that he was fierce of heart. By God, our righteous Father, I conjure you all here to speak. Tell me the whole truth. I would hear how he came to his death, my dear son, who lies here, and for whom my heart sorely grieves."

Then they all said, "it was a stranger, a knight who did this by his great valor. Though we did not see it with our own eyes, we came across the battle afterwards. So all we may bear witness to is that the stranger killed many of our folk, and wounded others so sorely that they may never be healed."

But Sir Gawain knew well that he was guilty, and saw that he could not escape there, since he had laid aside his weapons and stood unarmed in his robes. This troubled him no small amount.

At this moment the blood of the dead knight began to flow freely again, and ran crimson down the hall toward Sir Gawain. With this, the folk noticed Sir Gawain for the first time. Now all exclaimed that the one who killed the lord's son must be in the hall, for the blood had stopped flowing a little after midday, and no one had seen the wounds bleed since. Now the wounds reopened. Looking upon all present, they saw that Sir Grawain, the Father of Adventure, was the only stranger in the hall, and looked upon him with fierce and cruel eyes.

Seeing so many unfriendly faces turned toward him, Sir Gawain grew alarmed.

The folk then prayed to their lord that he would make this knight known to them: how did he come there, who was he, where did he come, where was he going, and what was his name?

The host said, "he is my guest. He has my safe conduct, good and fast, while he is within my castle. Make you sure of this, for if any wrong is done to him by word or deed, it will cost you your goods and life. I will not change my word for any prayer of man or woman: my surety will hold to every guest so fast that no word I have spoken will be broken with my knowledge or will. Have patience and hold you still, on peril of your lives and goods, and I will know if you secretly break my command: I will not have the shame of being known to break my word."

Having ensured Sir Gawain heard this and was at ease, he spoke quietly to his folk: "Be assured, I will avenge him more discreetly, if I am now well assured of the truth that my guest has indeed wrought this murder and great outrage! Now, do as I command. You will wait here in this hall. No man will follow me. I will lead my guest without the walls and you will close the door behind us. If my dead son stops bleeding, then we will all be well-assured he has done the deed. Thereafter, I will take counsel on how to avenge my son - but fittingly, and without shame."

Then the host approached Sir Gawain and addressed him. "Sir Knight, do not be angry that my folk treat you this way. We are in grief, as you see, and therefore you are the worse served. Now you will come with me, and I will amend what has been here lacking. My folk and household make great lamentation, as you see, and I with them. Now come with me and tarry not, I will lead you from here where you will be more at ease, and sleep softly until the daylight while we here moan and grieve."

Sir Gawain was led to a room in a strong tower whose walls were bare of weapons, and saw that he was entirely vulnerable. He considered his position, and could think of no better plan than to simply put himself in his host's grace and do what he was asked. In the room were comfortable beds, and this confirmed his host's honor, and suggested he might indeed be safe. Yet he had no weapon, and inside the castle were more than 500 armed men. When they were alone, his host spoke to him, saying "Sir Knight, and dear guest, be comfortable here tonight." He left Sir Gawain with many squires, for his service - or perhaps as his guard. But whether they were guarding Sir Gawain from the folk of the castle, or keeping him for those folk, could not be said as yet.

Meanwhile, in the hall the dead man was taken from where he laid, his wounds were stanched and he bled no more. Then they were all well assured that their guest had slain him. The host left the hall and returned to visit his guest, saying nothing. He locked the door of the tower fast, so that none would do Sir Gawain harm - and also to keep Sir Gawain in the tower. What could Sir Gawain do? He had come there as a guest, now was a captive, bare of arms. Though he was sorely troubled, he was not afraid. Yet he was troubled by what he could do - or rather by what he couldn't do. So did the constraint and misfortune male the night seem long.

The night was long for his host, as well. Sorrow and lamentation passed the night, for though the evil knight had deserved his death, none were willing to admit that he was evil, and cruel of heart. In the morning, the Lord took counsel on what to do. He was advised that if he let his guest, now held there captive, depart in safety, men would say he was a coward and dare not avenge himself, and the lord would become scorned. Yet if he were to slay his guest, especially after promising him safety, he would also be shamed in every land.

So it was decided that the lord would escort Sir Gawain safely to the borders of his lands, armed as he had come, and then return to his castle - and that his folk would then waylay Sir Gawain. Perhaps they would slay him, but they would try to capture him and deal with him as they might think best: perhaps they would burn him alive to cool their rage, or break him upon the wheel. But in any case, their lord would be relieved of any shame for harming his guest, or allowing his son to go unavenged. This plan pleased everyone well, and they departed to prepare ambushes to waylay Sir Gawain, no matter what direction he turned when he was released at the borders of their lands.

The King's servants did more than this though: when it came time to bring Sir Gawain his armor and weapons, they secretly replaced his good sword with a bad one that wasn't worth a shilling, they cut the straps of the harness and made a cut in the stirrups that would make them break at the first time they were used in battle. In many other ways they sabotaged Sir Gawain. But they did not harm his horse, for they thought that soon the horse would be their own after Sir Gawain was killed.

After they wrought this treason, they brought everything to Sir Gawain, they helped him get ready to depart. When he was ready, the lord of the castle came to Sir Gawain and invited him to eat breakfast and hear mass before he departed.

Sir Gawain answered, "my dear host, I grieve that you so sorrow for your son. God guard me and bring me to His grace when I die, I do truly mourn your misfortune. However, though it is hard and painful to me to say, for you have received me so well, yet I would nevertheless tell you the truth, and I would not deny it to any man, however strong he may be. Your son merited his death many times over. God have mercy upon him! And God reward you for the great good, and honor, that you have done to me. God reward all you here!"

His host was angered by these words, but remained outwardly calm. "I will do you no harm despite all that you have done to me. Nevertheless, there are many men here who would have fallen upon you before now, and I will not have them harm you now. So I will ride with you, and keep you from harm.

Gawain replied, "for this, may God reward you." He took his bridle in his hand and rode forth, his host very near to him, and the King's servants who had betrayed him at his side. Now Sir Gawain understood he had safe conduct, but did not know his sword had been stolen from him, or that the sword in his sheath was as brittle as grass, or the other sabotage he had suffered. He did not know that he was to be ambushed. Sir Gawain did not know he would soon be overmatched by the cowards in some way or another (for that is the way of cowards, attacking with surprise and at unfair advantage), and so he was unafraid, and talked of many things with his host.

When they came near the ambush, the King took his leave of Sir Gawain and returned to the castle. Sir Gawain thought he could ride

forth without a fight. But when he put his hand upon his saddlebow
and thrust his feet into his stirrups, thinking to rise in the saddle, the
girths broke, the saddle turned over beneath the horse and left him
on the ground. By skill, Sir Gawain landed on his feet. He then saw a
great company spring forth and come toward him with all their
might - some came from the ditches where they were hidden, some
came out of the bushes and thickets, some came from the hollows.

Sir Gawain saw he was betrayed and overmatched, and prayed to
God, that God might confound the traitors - for there was nothing he
himself might do against them. Nevertheless, bravely, he drew his
sword from his sheath to defend himself, as he had many a time
before. But before he could smite three blows his sword broke as if
it were tin - because it was. This was not a promising beginning to a
battle in which a man defend his life.

Sir Gawain was dismayed, he knew just then how much he had
been betrayed. They came from every side, a great company and
fierce, all thirsting for his life. Their swords clashed, their spars
thrusted. His sword broken, he dropped it into the sand and faced
his enemies empty handed. Like a wild boar defends himself against
the hounds Sir Gawain defended himself, but like the boar, his
courage came to nothing. It was the spears which harmed him most,
for he took hold of the swords. Nevertheless, though he killed some,
and wounded others beyond healing, he was overcome: there does
not live a man ever so strong or valiant who cannot be overcome by
force or fraud. Sir Gawain fell to the ground. And though he had

been betrayed by these cowards, he nevertheless, however wrongly, felt shame. But his wounds and pride would one day be healed.

To humiliate him, they bound Sir Gawain's hands, and set him on a sorry hack, leading him beside Gringalet. This they did to make him more grieved, and show him he had lost his horse. They told him they would make him die a shameful death. They swore oaths they would break him on the wheel. Some wanted to take Sir Gawain back to King Arthur's court to greater shame him, but then they decided it would be better to hang him by the neck at King Arthur's borders, so that all of King Arthur's court would avoid their lands and know the fate of those who would meddle in their affairs.

So they brought him back to the hermitage at the crossroads where a day earlier he, Sir Lancelot and Sir Morien had gone separate ways. Sir Gawain, grimly, reflected that not everything had gone awry, for at least he would at least be able to keep his promise to return to the crossroads when his adventure had ended.

But now I will leave speaking of Sir Gawain, and tell how it fared with Sir Morien on his way to the sea.

Sir Morien at the Sea

Sir Morien left the crossroads and rode the seaward road, and came safely to the beach. All that day he met no man of whom he might ask concerning his father. He thought it was labor lost, for all who saw him fled from him before he could take off his helmet to greet them politely, thinking he had come to rob them. But he saw hoof prints of horses before him that were newly made, and by this he deemed that his father had passed that way but a short while before him. Yet when he reached the sea, he lost the tracks in the sand.

That night he had no rest or sleep, for he had found no place where he might ask for food or lodging. Nor had he found any place to shelter upon the beach.

In the early morning, as soon as he could see well enough, he explored the nearby countryside. He found that robbers had laid waste to the land, and driven away the folk that lived there until none remained. This he thought explained the fears of those people he had met the previous day. Exploring about he found all the fields of the land had returned to the heath and sand, it had been a long time since it had been planted in wheat or barley.

Up and down the coast he saw or heard no man, nor any folk coming or going, but at last he did see some ships at anchor and shipmen upon the beach who waited to take folk to those boats, and then across the sea to Ireland. He approached them, and took off his helmet, politely greeting them, and asking "has any ship these last few days carried a knight over the water?"

But when these sailors saw his skin was black, they were afraid and astonished, for they had never seen or even heard of anyone having skin that color, and thought he must be a demon or even the Devil himself, scorched black from the fires of hell. So they fled from him, and they would not listen to anything he said, thinking his very words would enchant them and tempt them to evil.

But because of the swiftness of their flight, Sir Morien did not understand their thoughts, and believed they simply would not take him over the waters because he was a Moor. Alone on the beach, having eaten or drank nothing since he left the hermitage, he spoke quietly to himself. "What does it profit a man to labor if he knows it to be in vain? None will take me over the water because I am a Moor, and look differently than the people of these lands, or else flee before me, thinking I am one of those who have robbed them. My journey has been for nothing. I may do no better than to return to the Hermit, and await my comrades."

The Rescue of Sir Gawain

Looking about him one last time, Sir Morien saw no one in sight, no man or woman, nor indeed any animal, upon the shore. So, hungry, thirsty and dismayed, he turned backward upon his trail, and left the ocean behind him, and saw no one on his entire journey until he came within sight of the hermitage.

There, he saw a great number of armed folk in haulberks, directing carpenters who were cutting and shaping timber, making a great wheel. Looking closer, he saw a knight sitting upon the ground, bound, naked, covered in blood, and in sore distress and understood he had been brought there to be broken upon the wheel.

Sir Gawain noticed Sir Morien approaching and called aloud to him so all might hear, "Dear comrade! You are most welcome! Thank God for giving me the joy of seeing you come here. I am Gawain, your comrade! And little did I foresee this mischance when we parted, you and I, at this crossroad yesterday. Have pity upon me, may God strengthen you, that you might here show His power!"

Sir Morien did not hesitate a moment, but rode to Gawain's rescue without a single word in answer. Yet though he smote men left and right, his sword could neither dent nor scar their armor. Seeing this, he decided to rely instead on his great strength, and thereby broke and damaged all who stood against him with such ghastly wounds that none of them would ever be fully healed, tearing them limb from limb. Then, taking their own better swords to use against them, he was able to cleave their heads through their helmets to the teeth. Fortunately, Sir Morien was able to deflect all their blows and suffered no injuries. He felled them by twos and threes, some under their horses, some beside them.

During this battle, Sir Gawain sat on the side of the road with his hands bound in a sorry plight unable to do anything. But so evil was his situation, so bad were his hurts, that every time Sir Morien saw him there, his anger, courage and strength grew, so in this way Sir Gawain was at least able to encourage Sir Morien.

At last, Sir Morien drove back the folk, and the space began to widen between Sir Gawain and Sir Morien and those who would still dare to attack him. For it seemed to all their enemies that Sir Morien had come forth from hell and was the Devil himself, so harshly had he quelled and felled them underfoot, and so unable were they to trouble him with their own blows. In this way he was very much like his father, Sir Agloval.

Sir Morien said no word during this fighting, but smote blow after blow upon any who came near him. He was not even fatigued by this fighting, it was as if he were cutting grass or reeds. He spared neither horse nor man, and soon he was standing in a pool of blood, with heads and hands and arms and legs, and even entire men cut in half lying about him.

Now the folk began to flee without daring their combat with Sir Morien, and their cowardice put others to rout. Many of these had lost their horses to Sir Morien, and so they had a long journey ahead of them back to their own lands on foot.

When the field was won, Sir Morien dismounted and took Sir Gawain in his arms, and unbinding him said, "alas, my comrade, how were you thus betrayed? I fear there is no physician who can help you, you've been wounded so badly and so many times!"

Now freed, Sir Gawain, his heart light, smiled, laughed and assured him, "I have no need of a physician if I can rest but a couple days. By my own leechcraft and the help of certain herbs I will soon regain all my strength and be able to walk and ride again." He then thanked both Morien and God a hundred times that he was delivered from peril, and comforted in his need.

Now they found Gringalet. He was bare of harness and saddle, and the one who had been holding him back from helping Sir Gawain lay dead upon the grass, killed by the horse who would not permit itself to be mounted during the escape. Beside him were many other horses, the masters of whom had been killed, or fled on foot, and who had gathered themselves to Gringalet. And when Sir Gawain saw Gringalet, he forgot all his pain, and rose from where he sat, and went to his horse - and when Gringalet saw Sir Gawain, the horse rushed toward him, and nibbled him lovingly. Both horse and man were incredibly happy.

Then neither Sir Gawain nor Sir Morien saw any reason to remain in that place any longer but went to the hermitage. There, the hermit had been watching the battle from his window, and recognized the two knights from the day before. And when he heard their tale, and all that had happened to them, he spoke to Sir Gawain, the Father of Adventure, saying "I told you this would happen if you

rode that way! And I did ask you to not go! But you wouldn't listen
to me. And thereby came to great harm. Those who would despise
advice often do themselves a great mischief. But since things have
happened this way, I will give you more advice and urge you to stay
the night here with me, since you will not find any shelter nearer and
you will need shelter against that evil beast I spoke of when you were
here before. But you will probably do what you think is best anyhow.
You may not actually be much safer here than anywhere else, the
only reason I don't flee from the beast is because I do not fear death,
and I will not break the rules of my religious order. My own story is
long, and a long story is hard to hear when you are already weary - if
you stay here, I will do what I can to see you are not lacking to your
ease. Stable your steeds, and spend the night here with me in my
chapel. That which I have I will share with you, for the love of God
and the honor of your knighthood!"

Sir Gawain and Sir Morien thanked the hermit very much, and
took his advice. Stabling their horses, they went to the chapel, and
there they told each other of their adventures. The hermit tended
the horses well, and bade the lad who served him to bring forth food,
and fetch water from the spring, and warm it for Sir Gawain so he
might bathe his wounds more comfortably. Searching his wounds, it
was seen that Sir Gawain had suffered nothing mortal thanks to his
hauberk - otherwise he would have certainly died from the many
blows he had received.

At the Hermitage

After Sir Gawain was tended to, Sir Gawain and the Hermit rejoined Sir Morien in the chapel and the three spoke at length on many things. And the hermit told them he had heard from pilgrims shortly after Sir Lancelot, Sir Gawain and Sir Morien left that the Red Knight and his companions had in fact just lately ridden the road to the sea.

Sir Morien told the Hermit he had followed the fresh hoof prints until he came to the sea crossing into Ireland, and there lost the tracks, and could get no information from the sailors there. "Howsoever I might ask them, when they saw me they were terrified as rabbits, the fools. All of them fled and put out to sea! By the faith I owe to God and Our Lady, and the honor of knighthood, learning what you just told me their fear will avail them nothing. I will return to the sea, and make them one of them to take me to Ireland. He will certainly think he was born in an evil hour, for if he will not carry me over the water I will threaten to kill him. I fear the knight you spoke of is my father, and I have missed him. I will follow hard after him, but will take your advice, Hermit, and await the dawn. I do not think he could have rode so far ahead of me. I will not be able to overtake him, if my horse, who is strong and fast, does not fail me."

"God speed you," said Sir Gawain, whose thoughts now turned to his own evil plight. He lamented that his good sword had been stolen from him, and his saddle destroyed, and his heart was heavy. Besides having no armor, he had no clothes, either! But, before bed,

Sir Gawain treated his own wounds again, and saw all of them were already beginning to heal, so he took some comfort.

That night they spent well, and the Hermit ensured they lacked nothing. At dawn, Sir Gawain was troubled that he lacked arms and clothing, and his wounds, though healing, hurt him more. And they had eaten all the Hermit's food, nor was there anyone near at hand who might give them more, even if they had money to buy it with: it would be seven miles of hard riding to the nearest village in Arthur's land. Sir Gawain was of a mind to ride in search of Sir Lancelot, to learn what had befallen of him. Yet he could not yet ride his horse, and so he would have to wait a day or more at the hermitage.

Sir Morien's heart was set upon following his father, but thought it would be shameful to abandon his comrade, Sir Gawain, leaving him vulnerable and wounded. So he stayed with him in the chapel.

As Morien stood by the window deep in thought, he saw a knight riding fast toward the hermitage. The knight was well armed. He remarked to Sir Gawain, "what is this? A knight rides toward the hermitage, and I do not know where he goes!"

Gawain got up with difficulty and approached the window with more difficulty still. When he looked upon the knight, he saw it was Sir Garlet, his brother of both father and mother! He rode fast from the road that led to Arthur's lands. Now Sir Gawain was happier than I can tell you, for Sir Garlet was strong and valiant, and brought with him all they lacked: bread, meat, and wine, fresh and clear!

When Sir Garlet came to the hermitage, Sir Gawain came forth from the chapel, shouting "God give you good day, brother! Never was I so joyful since I was born!"

Sir Garlet dismounted, and it was clear that he was troubled. For in Britain they lost King Arthur, and were in danger of losing all their land, and so they had sent Sir Garlet to seek for Sir Gawain and Sir Lancelot, the most valiant and unmatched knights of the court. Yet when Sir Garlet saw the sorry state his brother Sir Gawain was in, he forgot these troubles and was troubled anew: "alas, brother, how did this happen to you? It will be a miracle if you are healed, and live, so badly you are wounded!"

Sir Gawain tried to reassure his brother, "true, I do not have a limb that isn't wounded and hurts, but I am whole of heart and will heal myself well enough. But let that tale be for now. You looked troubled when you arrived, before you saw me - tell me why you rode here?"

Sir Garlet said he would tell him. So they went into the chapel, where they found the Hermit and Sir Morien.

Sir Garlet, seeing Sir Morien was black in face and limb, was surprised! When this surprise wore off, he looked at him closer, and saw he was a great and good man. Yet, never having heard of anyone with skin of that color, Sir Garlet was astonished, and filled with wonder. Seeing his brother speechless, Sir Gawain introduced him to Sir Morien, and told him who he was, and where he came.

So the four sat down together, and made joy of their meeting. But soon Sir Gawain asked his brother what brought him there. Sir

Garlet said the worst had befallen, "King Arthur is taken captive! He was hunting in the forest as he often did, and there came upon the King the greatest company of armed men I might tell you of. They were all men of the King of the Saxons. They were in such force they took King Arthur. No one foresaw any of this, and the King had few folk with him when he went hunting. We are all troubled, the Queen most of all. She does not know where these Saxons took him, but the forest stands by the sea and it might be that he has been taken over it. But we have another woe besides: the Irish King has come into the land, and made war. One town he has already won, and lays siege to another. He boasts he will win all of Arthur's lands, hill and vale, castle and town, and bring it all under his hand. The Queen is afraid, for it does not seem we can withstand them. Had you, my brother, and Perceval, and Lancelot been in the land we would have never come to such a desperate situation. But my lady the Queen has taken counsel, and sent messengers far and near to every land to seek for you and Lancelot in her need. I am one of those messengers, and rode as quickly as my horse might bear me from Arthur's court to here. I have heard tidings of you, and learned you came to this crossroads. I was told it was remote and I would find no man or woman and so I prepared myself and brought food, meat and bread, so I would not need of them, and also cool clear wine in flasks hereby my saddle - that I might lay my hand on them when I needed them!"

At this, Sir Gawain laughed and said he had properly prepared and come just in time, since they indeed had no food or wine. It seemed that while Sir Garlet doubted and brought food and wine, God provided for Sir Gawain, Sir Morien and the Hermit, who had not!

Sir Garlet answered, "well, then, let us eat and drink, for it seems we need to. But where is Sir Lancelot? I do not see him here."

Sir Gawain explained that he had rode from the hermitage to seek Sir Percival.

"You vex yourselves to seek him, it is labor lost: tidings have come to court that Sir Percival has become a hermit, and does penance for his sins. He learned that even if he sought until Judgement Day the spear and grail, he would never find them. For he sinned against his mother when he left her in the forest, and that sin hindered him, so even if he did find them, he could not win them. He must be pure, and clean from all stain and sin if he would have the spear and grail. For sorrow at this Sir Percival betook himself to a hermitage, and sent word to the court that he did so. And concerning his brother, Sir Agloval, the messenger said he lays sick with his uncle, sorely wounded, but it seemed likely he would recover. So let us now eat, Sir Gawain, and go on our way to the Queen with honor: this my Lady the Queen requires of you and Sir Lancelot, upon your faith to her. But I am frustrated that Sir Lancelot escaped me!"

When Sir Morien, son of Sir Agloval, heard this, he asked if Sir Garlet could tell him where his uncle had made his hermitage, and where his father lay wounded?

Sir Garlet said, "if you had a boat and a favorable wind, you could get there quickly: about 15 miles from here, there is a sea crossing.

Go over the arm of the sea, and when you cross it, on the far shore at the landing there is a forest. It seems that it may be the greatest forest in the world, and the wildest. It is certainly long and wide, but the hermitage is within it but a short distance, perhaps a mile."

Morian was excited. "So help me God, I will be there soon. And with some good luck I will even see my father there. And before I depart from him he will keep the vow he swore to my mother when he left her sorrowing, that he would wed her and make her his wife! Even if he is in fear of death, he will keep his oath and ride with me to the Moorish lands." With this, he got up and prepared to leave.

Sir Garlet replied, "if God wills, things will turn out for you even better than you hope between your father and you. We will eat and drink before we depart, and if you are wise, you might think to do the same if you will be any good to your father when you arrive. I ask you, by the faith that you owe to our Lady, and the honor of knighthood, that you do as I ask, and let your thoughts be of good, and not evil, and heed the wisdom Sir Gawain told you before - then no harm will befall you."

Morien paused, and considered, and then agreed.

At this, Sir Garlet brought forth a tablecloth, white and clean,and spread it before the knights (as befits noble folk and those worthy of honor). He then brought forth seven loaves of white bread, and laid them upon the table. Then was brought forth ham and venison, and clear wine - two bottles full. It was quite welcome to those who partook of it, and through these victuals they forgot all their troubles. They were happy at the table, these three knights and the hermit.

When the meal was ended, Sir Morien was about to depart when Sir Garlet asked him to wait, "Sir Knight, you can do better than depart in haste. Consider, if you do, you will have trouble finding your father. It is now early afternoon, and if you do come safely to the ships before they depart, it would be over late before you come to the other side."

Sir Gawain agreed with this wise counsel. "Knight, I will tell you what to do. From haste rarely comes that which abides honor. Therefore, tarry overnight with us, since you cannot achieve your goal today, and I will make my weapons ready as best I may. I must myself be better healed before I have strength to ride to battle, but tomorrow I will be able to ride with you to the shore, without delay, at sunrise. I have no mind to hinder you or cause you delay, but there are enemies near at hand who have wrought me harm, and who may do you more harm than they did me."

Sir Morien thought upon this, and also how Sir Gawain might help him secure passage with the sailors who might not be afraid of him, and agreed readily.

Throughout the night, while Morien spoke of his many adventures, Sir Gawain prepared his harness and weapons, sharpening and polishing them, testing them. But he still sorrowed for his good sword that he had lost.

What do I gain by making my tale longer? The next day dawned, shedding beauty over hill and vale, and the three knights rode forth together. They did not spare themselves. And Sir Gawain told Sir Garlet that he would seek Sir Lancelot before returning to the court of King Arthur, since he might not well with honor return without him, or learning how it had gone for him: and he was curious to learn what adventures Sir Lancelot had. Would God prosper him, he would bring Sir Lancelot with him to the aid of the Queen, and on this his mind was set, nor would he do otherwise, for any man's prayer.

Sir Garlet was ill pleased, and said Sir Gawain would do better to return quickly, and take the place of his uncle, King Arthur, and care for the Kingdom, its land and folk. He had responsibilities as the heir! But this Sir Gawain would not do, his mind already made up. So Sir Garlet gave him his sword, which was good and bright, and they took leave of each other, and the Hermit.

Sir Garlet and Sir Morien kept Sir Gawain company for a mile, and then Sir Gawain told his brother to return to the Queen, telling her he would return to her quickly, and in good faith and loyalty. But that it would not profit Sir Garlet anything to keep Sir Gawain further company. So did Sir Garlet and Sir Morien turn aside, commending Sir Gawain to the care of God and all His saints, and so did he them. Each saw tears spring from their eyes and run down their beards as they parted. I cannot tell you how often and warmly Sir Gawain thanked Sir Morien, that he saved his life on the field where he would have surely been killed had God not sent that good knight to his aid.

When Sir Morien and Sir Garlet parted from Sir Gawain, they rode once more back to the crossroads to keep the compact they made that they should not part until they found Sir Agloval together, and that Sir Morien would ask his uncle and father to come to the aid of the Queen and help her win back her lands.

As they rode to the ships at the shore, Sir Morien confessed he was worried that even with Sir Garlet with him, the sailors would again flee from him since they feared him and would certainly recognize him.

Sir Garlet agreed this was likely, and suggested that he should ride ahead of Sir Morien, so as to arrive at the shore well ahead of Sir Morien so as to hire a ship for them both. "Don't arrive too quickly, but wait until you see that I am on a ship, and the boatman is in my power: I will make sure he does not depart before you can board. I won't let him free before he has taken us to the farther shore. Even if he would want to leave you behind, I will ensure he knows it will be better for him to been sunk and drowned in the sea."

Sir Morien thought this was good, "you have found the best counsel that may be devised. I will do as you advise."

So Sir Garlet rode alone until he came to the ships, and found a boat that was good and strong, pleasing him well. He offered the boatman enough money to take him to the far side without delay. And, taking gold in hand, he made his sails and rigging ready - and this he soon regretted, for even as Sir Garlet had come on board and was ready for the crossing, Sir Morien came riding across the beach. Sir Morien was blacker than any son of man whom the sailor's eyes had ever beheld, and he wanted to flee when he beheld the black knight. He was so scared that he could not move a limb, and thought he might die of fear.

Now Sir Garlet asked the sailor, "Sir boatman, what ails you? By Heaven, you will ferry us both over swiftly. Now, make no ado or this will be your last day!" The sailor was still scared stiff. Sir Garlet attempted to persuade him, arguing with his fear: "by the Lord who made us, what are you afraid of? This man is not the devil! He just has dark skin! He is 14 years old. He has never even seen Hell. He is my comrade. Let him in!"

Still unable to move, the sailor did not respond. Sir Garlet used his weapons to persuade the sailor, "I counsel you straightly, Sir boatman!" This argument the boatman had to obey, though he did not like it.

As soon as he had in his boat Sir Morien he saw indeed he was no devil, but a man. But he was still afraid, for Sir Morien was such a huge man, and his horse seemed over strong. And he was all the while threatened by Sir Garlet. So he pushed his boat from shore and put out to sea, fearing that he would be lost that day.

When underway, Sir Morien took off his helmet and the boatman saw his face was black. The boatman thought he was a dead man, and begged mercy, for (so he thought) such a dark man certainly could be no Christian. All the while, Sir Garlet interrogated the boatman, asking news of the two knights who had passed that way, one of whom rode a red horse and wore red armor, the other wearing the badge of King Arthur. Sir Garlet told the boatman if he could tell them anything, that he would give the boatman great thanks.

The boatman said, "it is not very long since they were in my boat - the one knight wore red armor and had with him a red horse, the other was wounded and bore King Arthur's badge. And I know by the same badge that you are yourself one of King Arthur's knights. They would both cross over, and I ferried them to the far side. It was to them an unknown land, that I overheard from their talking. I thought they were ill at ease, but I did not know why. I saw that one wept so that the tears fell thick down his face, and when I brought them to the other side, the one knight asked me if there was a hermitage nearby where a hermit lived? So I showed it to him."

This tale and more they heard before they touched the sand on the far shore. Then Sir Garlet made the boatman show them where this hermitage was, but the boatman refused and would only show them the road to it. So they left the boatman, who was very happy to be rid of them. The knights went on their way to the hermitage.

When they arrived, they dismounted, and secured their horses by the door. Crying with a loud voice to those within, they shouted "let us in! Open of your good will!" a boy came to the door and asked what they wanted, or if they needed help?

Sir Morien again permitted Sir Garlet to speak for him. Sir Garlet said that if it were pleasing to the Hermit and Sir Agloval, they would talk with them. At this the boy said he would relay the request to the Hermit and Sir Agloval, and went on his way. Sir Garlet in this way confirmed that Sir Agloval was indeed at the hermitage.

The boy reported to Sir Agloval and the Hermit two knights stood outside and wanted to talk to them. "They both are handsome, and well armed, but one of them - his armor and his limbs (so far as I could see) are blacker than soot or pitch. I do not know their errand, but they wanted to speak with you." Sir Morien's dark skin did not cause anyone at the hermitage to be alarmed.

Sir Agloval, who thought this very strange, went to the gate as best he could, and the Hermit followed. Sir Agloval looked through the wicket and saw Sir Garlet, Sir Gawain's brother, and recognized him: for Sir Garlet was himself worthy of great honor, even though never so much as his brother Sir Gawain.

When Sir Garlet saw Sir Agloval, they gave each other fair and courteous greetings. "May He who can do all things show favor and honor to you, Sir Knight, and to all who be with you there within!"

Sir Agloval looked upon Sir Morien, and saw he was a Moor, and was surprised. At that moment, seeing Sir Agloval's recognition, Sir Morien stood before Sir Agloval and asked him, "do you remember how, in seeking for Sir Lancelot, you came to the land of the Moors, and how there you loved a maiden, and promised to marry her, and how she granted you her favors before you departed on your quest? Have you ever thought about her after you left that land, or remembered your promise to return as soon as may be to marry her, for her profit and her honor? Do you now think upon these things?"

Sir Agloval made his answer, "Sir Knight, I make no denial, but I have seldom been a rest. I rode in the quest of Sir Lancelot for a while, and thereafter could not return, for then I had brought my brother back to court, where he was held in high honor. And so soon as he was made a knight, I was required to ride with him upon a journey which he would delay for no reason, for he was eager to avenge the harm done to our father many years ago. This you must understand? My brother knew well that our enemies had taken themselves the hermitage that should have been ours when they drove our father forth from it. This he would avenge, and we have had much fighting before we might regain it. But just now we have done so, and slain all those who possessed themselves of our land. That so many years have fled since I swore to the maiden I would return to her came of necessity. Now, I do not deny that I have failed to keep my oath, and I must now think well upon what to do, and seek counsel in the matter. I do not know even whether that lady you speak of is living or dead, for I have heard nothing of her."

Morien replied, "then I shall tell you of her! She to whom you gave your word lives still, and is my mother, and you, Sir Knight, are my father! And I will counsel you in the matter: if you will come with me now, at her prayer and mine, then you will do well and courteously. You begat me upon her who should be your wife, had you kept your oath. Now consider what I have said well, and say if you will come or not."

Sir Agloval was quick to respond. "By Heaven, Sir Knight, I believe you, every word. That which she lays claim from me she is indeed owed, and I have betrayed her, and forsworn my oath. But I will make my word good by the help of God. I will yet win her grace and forgiveness! Come here within to my uncle and brother, they will counsel us well when they hear our tale - so shall we be more at ease!"

With that, Sir Agloval undid the wicket and it would have done any heart good to see Sir Agloval and Sir Morien embrace and kiss each other, and to hear such words of love and friendship they shared! And when Sir Perceval heard the story told by Sir Agloval and Sir Morien, he gave a glad welcome to his nephew, as did the hermit. And to honor Sir Morien, they brought forth such food and drink as was within the hermitage, and there was nothing but gladness as each made great joy of each other. And so they wearied themselves until it was time to sleep, and slept well until the day broke and the sun shone forth again.

Sir Agloval's Dream

The next day the knights slept longer than the hermit, who had to sing his prayers and mass before day dawned. When they had awakened and dressed, Morien told his father that he wished to ride now, and wanted to know if his father would come with him to his mother and do what he had promised when he departed from her? He told his father how they had been deprived of their rightful inheritance from his mother's father, "it was altogether denied her by the law of the land. Yet it was shame more than that loss which grieved her, for everyone called her son fatherless, as she could bring no proof of the promise she had received, nor show them the face of the man who was my father."

Sir Agloval promised Sir Morien he would give him an answer, but put the matter off for one reason or another all day. And while they stayed with the hermit, they were well served, and comfortable, but Morien pressed the matter again and again, saying he would leave now, and not delay, and needed to know if his father would keep his promise to his mother.

At last, Sir Agloval answered Sir Morien, and began by saying that he had had a vision in a dream: it seemed that they had rode throughout the day in a land where there was nothing but wilderness and woods, with trees, many and beautiful. After a while, they rode through hail, and then snow, and then through the heat of the noon so hot that it was painful. While he saw the sun shine bright, it was dark about him, as if the twilight had fallen. He saw all kinds of beasts in the forest, and folk, young and old, go up and down through the woods. All this he saw in his dream, but nowhere in his dream could he find a place in that land to find shelter.

Then, in his dream, as it drew toward evening, and the light failed, he thought he saw a tower, built so strong that no one by force could win their way within. Yet there was no doorway. However there was another tower that stood nearby. And within this he beheld a stairway which wound up to a door at the end. This door seemed to him as high as a church, and built of iron. If a man were sick, he might be healed by the light that streamed forth from within, for as he saw and looked upon it, it seemed that it might be Heaven! And every step of the stairway was made of rose gold.

He thought to himself, within the dream, that those stairs were so beautiful that he wanted to set his feet upon them, and learn how many there were, that hereafter he might speak more of the wonder he had seen. But when he counted sixty, and would set his foot upon the next, he saw none of those he had left below him (except the one upon which he stood) and none above him! It seemed to him that the door was distant from the step as high as one might shoot with a bow. Thus, he could go neither forward nor backward.

And then he beheld, on the ground beneath were now snakes and wild bears, and they wanted to tear him to pieces! They gnashed their teeth, as if to seize him, and gaped with their jaws as if to swallow him. It seemed as if they were at his heels as the snakes twisted themselves upward. And now, there were dragons below him as well!

Sir Agloval said of his dream, "and now I was afraid that the step might break beneath me, and I might fall down into the snakes, bears, and dragons! And I was so afraid that I had awakened, and could not sleep any more."

This dream, he said, worried him, and made him feel angry whenever he thought about it. He had no idea what it meant, but his heart forebode pain, and mischief, and difficult work lay ahead of him. Then, one day, he met with a learned clerk, and told him of this dream, and the clerk understood it well, and interpreted it. Agloval shared what he had learned from the clerk, saying "concerning our lands, great and small, that we should be in great distress and fear before we win them again. For strong were the castles and mighty the armies, therefore did the vision foretell ill to my brother and myself each and singly. And the clerk further spoke concerning my brother Perceval, and the Spear and the Grail: for that golden stairway betokened the Holy Grail, and that Percival should aid in the winning of it, but in doing so he would die. And the door that stood above and the stairway itself betokened the heavenly kingdom, as was known by the light that showed within. And the steps that lay before it counted the length of Percival's life. Each step might be a day, or a week, or a month, he did not know. But that the step broke beneath me was for my sins, and I might have ascended to heaven if my sins had not laid hold upon me. The bears, snakes and dragons that lay in wait for me - these are the fiends that my sins made, to carry me to Hell." So was Agloval counseled to take warning, and correct his ways with wisdom, and speedily, and not delay, for his time was coming, and soon.

"My dear son," spoke Agloval, "with this warning my brother ceased his quest for the Spear and Grail, and the adventure on which he was bound, and came here as quick as he could to my uncle, the hermit here, and clothed himself in this habit. Thus we are here together, for my brother would amend his life, and I am not yet whole enough to leave. I was wounded near to death, and so bruised and manhandled, that I must stay here a while with my brother and uncle for my wounds to be tended, and that with them I may save my soul. Now you would have me journey with you to your mother, and I would like to ride there if I were healed. But that is another matter besides: I would gladly go with you for your honor, and to do away your shame, were it not that I must now trust in my uncle to make my peace with God. Now, counsel me as it seems best to you, since I am your father."

Sir Morien replied, "were you better healed I would have you ride, but it would do me no good for you to come to harm or mischief. I can give you no other advice than to abide here until you are once again whole. King Arthur is captive and his land sore beset. Here is his nephew Sir Garlet, who came here with me, and now that I have learned the truth of you, my father, I shall ride with him to court to do him honor and there abide until you are whole and healed. And I will return here in the hour that I know you to be cured of your wounds, and may keep the oath you swore to my mother, and thereby be better praised among men and find favor with God. Then my mother will once more be possessed of her lands she was disinherited from, and has for a long time lacked. May all good befall you here, I shall depart and aid the Queen, and God grant I may win such fame as shall be for the bettering of her cause and my own honor and profit. I shall return, be sure of it, and will until then think of you as my father."

All those there agreed this was the best course of action, and no better advice might be found. So Sir Garlet and Sir Morien asked Sir Perceval if he would ride with them, to aid the Queen and release King Arthur, and comfort his land. And this Sir Perceval agreed to do if his uncle would grant him leave to do so. Then all of them, Sir Agloval with them, prayed the uncle to grant that request, and you might never again see any folk so blithe as were these knights in asking that Sir Perceval be allowed to ride with them! Thus did they take their leave and wend on their way.

But now I will leave speaking of them and tell how it fared with Sir Lancelot.

The Adventure of Sir Lancelot

When Sir Lancelot departed from Sir Gawain and Sir Morien at the crossroads he rode for an hour until he came to the wilderness wasteland where the beast had wrought havoc.

Now, in that land there was a maiden who made it known far and wide that whosoever could slay the beast she would take for her husband. Never might a man behold a more beautiful maiden, and all that land was in her power! But there was also a traitorous knight who lived in that land as well: he loved this maiden, but could not slay the beast, so he kept watch upon the beast so that if any man should slay it he might slay the slayer and claim the deed for himself.

Sir Lancelot rode through the wilderness wasteland, seeking for the beast. He was able to track it and find the place it had made its lair. There he saw many helmets, spears and weapons of the knights it had slain, their bones lay on the ground stripped of flesh. It was clear the monster had devoured these men, and even Sir Lancelot was afraid to see this.

Sir Lancelot looked closely, and determined where the beast was likely to be lying in rest, and rushed toward it. As soon as the beast became aware of his coming, it rushed to meet Sir Lancelot! It feared neither sword nor spear nor any might of man, nor was it bothered by armor. And though Lancelot smote the monster so his spear broke in two, he had not even so much as bruised it, or scratched its hide. So then he drew his sword and smote it with great force, but he couldn't harm the beast.

The beast now took hold of Sir Lancelot by the throat and tore a great rent through the hauberk into his flesh. This made Sir Lancelot angry, but though Sir Lancelot struck and smote the beast many times, he could not harm it at all and the beast continued its attack upon him. The beast cut every part of his body, even his feet, and breathed out venom upon him.

Truly, had it not been for the magic ring Sir Lancelot wore upon his finger he would have fallen dead where he stood from the poison. The ring was called "Dispeller," and was given to him by the Lady of the Lake, the fairy who was his foster mother. It had the power to protect him from harm, and free him from all spells and help him see through magical illusions, as well as to cast illusions sufficient for Sir Lancelot to disguise himself if needed, and to call upon his foster mother for help.

Now the monster became aware of Sir Lancelot's enchantment, and sprang toward him with gaping jaws to swallow him whole. This Sir Lancelot saw as his chance, and so he thrust his sword into its mouth, cleaving its heart in two. The beast gave such a terrible cry it could be heard two miles away!

This the traitor heard, and rushed quickly to the lair, understanding the beast had been slain at last. When he came to the place he found Sir Lancelot sitting, binding his wounds, which were many and deep. This the traitor saw as his chance, and riding up to Sir Lancelot, offered to help him. Sir Lancelot was glad for the help, and while disarming and unarmoring Sir Lancelot to better bind his wounds, the traitor took hold of Sir Lancelot's sword and struck him, wounding Sir Lancelot so that he fell down to die.

When the traitor saw that Sir Lancelot would soon die, he went to the monster, and cut off the right foot, thinking to take it to the maiden, that with it he might win her as his wife.

But at this very moment, Sir Gawain, who had been tracking Sir Lancelot - even as Sir Lancelot had been tracking the beast - arrived at the lair of the beast. Seeing the traitor cut off the foot of the beast with Sir Lancelot's sword, and Sir Lancelot laying dying, Sir Gawain rode fast and rushed at the traitor shouting, "Stand still, Sir Murderer, for this beast's foot you have slain my comrade - this I see right well!" The traitor would have fled, but Sir Gawain was so near that he couldn't. Sir Gawain, for his part, didn't hesitate but seeing the traitor thinking about fleeing, struck him down. At this, the traitor begged mercy.

Sir Gawain decided he would bring the traitor to Sir Lancelot for judgment. Now, Sir Lancelot had, hearing Sir Gawain, had pulled himself up a little, and seeing Sir Gawain bringing him the traitor called out as loud as he might in his injury to Sir Gawain, telling him not to bother bringing the traitor to him. "Dear comrade, slay him now! I shall die the easier knowing that he is already dead. That traitor struck me while I was unarmed - even while unarming me under the guise of helping me with my injuries!" Sir Gawain obliged Sir Lancelot's dying wish, and did made no more ado but smote off the traitor's head.

Now he went quickly to Sir Lancelot, and bemoaned his injuries. "Sir Knight, can you be healed? Tell me the truth, I will help if I may." While Sir Gawain bound his wounds with herbs to stop the bleeding, Sir Lancelot told him how he had fared with the beast, but the injuries of the traitor's attack had wrought him the greater harm. "Yet if I can find a place nearby where I might rest, I do think I might be healed."

Sir Gawain took Sir Lancelot and set him upon his horse, and returned to the hermitage at the crossroads as best he might. Both thought if they could only get Sir Lancelot there, Sir Gawain might be able to save his life.

As they arrived, Sir Garlet and Sir Morien had just arrived back from Ireland with Sir Perceval and there was tremendous joy and gladness. The Hermit prepared food for his guests, and a couch for Sir Lancelot as best he might. Each told the other how matters had fallen out with them, but all wanted to hear most how things had fallen out with Sir Morien and his father first.

That night they enjoyed the Hermit's hospitality, but the next day as the knights continued to rest at the hermitage and share all that had happened since they last met, when Sir Lancelot heard how it had gone badly with the Queen, he would not be persuaded to rest any more. "Not even if I should gain the world thereby," he said he would not remain any longer. "Not for wounds nor weariness." He greatly desired to fight, and asked to leave first thing the next morning, asking Sir Gawain to continue to treat his wounds as they rode on their way.

The Rescue of Queen Guinevere

As they rode back to King Arthur's lands, they heard tidings that their lady, the Queen, was beset on all sides by the King of Ireland. He had burnt and laid waste to so much that the whole tale could not be told. The King of Ireland had even burned the churches of the land! There was no one left who was not a widow or an orphan and all the land was in terror.

The Queen was now beset in a castle under siege and the King of Ireland had sworn a great oath that if he would win the castle, he would ruin it, breaking it to the foundations, and spare no man within, but kill them, and their Queen, with such shame that men would speak of it for all time. He had sworn this by his crown, and all that might bind a King, and eagerly anticipated doing them bitter shame, burning them alive.

The castle was by a swift river, broad and deep. The castle was well designed. It was of gray hewn stone. It was the strongest castle of King Arthur's lands, but even still it would fall in a day. The folk within, knowing they would receive no mercy, were preparing to attempt a retreat from the castle the next day, rather than be burned alive there.

As the knights approached the castle, they saw the survivors of the desolation fleeing with what goods they might carry, for they had heard that even the women, children and old men would be burned alive. They drove their cattle before them, and though some were horsed, most were on foot.

Courteously speaking with the refugees, Sir Garlet learned that such a flight was the best they could do, according to their thinking, for they deemed they would certainly lose if they fought to defend themselves. "We lack leaders," they explained to Sir Garlet. "Sir Gawain and Sir Lancelot both have left the land, and we are without King or counsel."

Sir Morien asked the refugees if there were no leaders or counsel to be found in the castle, and why would they not flee toward it, rather than away?

The refugees answered that they had hoped the castle would have lasted seven years, but it seemed God had forsaken King Arthur and his lands, and those within were preparing to retreat. The King of Ireland would take the castle the next day, and slay all within, and all within the countryside about it, shamefully. "Since we may not hope for aid, we are forsaking the castle, and taking to flight."

Sir Gawain was kinder, and told the refugees he agreed that what they did did seem the best, and as they left, wished them well. "Good friends, God reward you for your tidings."

By back ways, the knights rode to and within the castle, and were warmly welcomed. They encouraged those within that God would bring the matter to a good ending, and there was great rejoicing over the coming of Sir Gawain and Sir Lancelot.

Then Sir Gawain introduced them to Sir Morien, and told all the young knight had done for them, and how he was one of the best knights the sun ever shone upon.

The folk of the castle saw him. Though he was not remarkable looking upon his horse, when he stood upon his feet they thought he might rout the entire army of the King of Ireland himself, he was so big.

Sir Morien, seeing he had their attention, then spoke to the folk in the castle, saying "it is good we are all here! It would be a sin and disgrace to yield the castle, and better to adventure our lives for the sake of the King our lord, and see the matter to an end." The words of Sir Morien seemed good to them, and they agreed.

Sir Gawain and Sir Lancelot also agreed, and Sir Gawain then spoke to all those within the castle, saying "here and now we may win fame for ourselves, and uphold the honor of our lord King Arthur. Though the King is still a captive, if God wills it he shall escape. My heart and mind tell me that if we only will hold out here it shall be to our honor! He who fails his King is rightly shamed before men and the world. Good fortune surely awaits us, and I have hope that heaven shall shortly send us help.

Now any doubts that lingered in the folk within the castle were put to rest, and none thought about escaping the battle they would fight the next day, but eagerly looked forward to it and all swore oaths they would never surrender.

Before the end of the day, the King of Ireland came before the castle and, together with many knights of his household, and many other folk besides, warlike, demanded of those within to surrender the castle. If they did, they would save their lives. But now everyone within had sworn to never surrender, and answered they would never betray their rightful lord. The King then swore an oath that if they did not surrender, they would never escape the uttermost that he might do to them. But for this threat they cared little, and made themselves ready for a last defense.

The folk within the castle thought to remain upon their battlements and throw from the castle such stones so great and heavy that the King should be driven from the walls out onto the open field where he had pitched his tents - and then they would be better able to attack him.

But as night fell, the Irish set up their tents and pavilions in the greenwood about the castle, and seeing this, the folk of the castle took counsel. They agreed that if they did not attack that night, or first thing in the morning, tomorrow would bring even more Irish about the castle and they'd be even more outnumbered than they were already.

Upon this, Sir Lancelot encouraged them all to not revel that night, but eat and drink enough to ready themselves. Not one man waivered that night as it drew toward morning, and as the day dawned they were all eager to do great deeds. Each looked to his armor as one who will fight for his life, and gave his horse a good feed of corn.

Why should I make this a longer tale? With the dawning of the day, all of them within the castle were ready, and armed and mounted on good horses. They undid the gates and rode forth in all their strength!

In the Irish camp, those who kept shield watch became aware of them, and led their company against the folk of the castle. But the Irish couldn't harm them! Sir Morien led the vanguard, and his weapons were too strong. No one had ever seen a man smite such strokes! Behind Sir Morien, they fought their way to and through the camp. Sir Gawain, Sir Perceval and Sir Lancelot smote many to death, and coming to the King's tent, seized the Irish weapons, shields and spears before they could even arm themselves. The Irish didn't know what befell them. No quarter would King Arthur's men give.

Those who were with the Irish King were sleeping soundly at the beginning of the attack, and awakening to see the stern intentions of King Arthur's knights tried to flee - but those who could were sorely wounded. And they were glad and blithe to escape with their lives.

The Irish King would have preferred to have been slain with all his folk, but was captured alive. And when the Irish King was captured, there was no man at his side.

They led the Irish King within the castle, and shut him fast in a tower. Never before had they housed a guest they were so welcome to receive!

The Irish fled as best they might, and neither took nor recked what they had brought with them to the camp. Such spoils were freely taken by the folk of the castle back with them. And when the battle was ended, many of the Irish who laid wounded were taken captive, together with their King.

The battle had gone well, but it was the dread of Sir Morien's mighty blows, and Sir Lancelot and Sir Gawain and Sir Perceval who had won the field, and brought the terror and dread of death to the Irish.

The Rescue of King Arthur

The folk of the castle hung out their shields upon the walls so that any Irish who would come to rescue their King might see they were ready to defend themselves. And when the Irish saw Sir Gawain's badge, and Sir Lancelot's pennon beside it, they drew off their forces and all those who served the Irish King were greatly shamed and asked Sir Gawain in what way they might make peace and obtain the return of their King?

Sir Gawain took counsel with his comrades, and this was their proposal: the Irish would bring King Arthur before their eyes, then terms might be made for peace, and the return of the King of Ireland.

Why should I make my tale overlong? Little as the Irish liked it, they knew they must bring King Arthur there and make terms.

When it became known that the King of Ireland had been taken captive, and that King Arthur was being brought to the castle, King Arthur's people were encouraged, and surrounding the Irish as they brought King Arthur forth, rescued the King their lord, taking him from the men of Ireland. They then brought King Arthur safely to the castle.

Thus did it fall out well for King Arthur.

When the King of Ireland saw King Arthur before him, and knew he had escaped and was free, he asked to see King Arthur straight away. He offered him goods and gold, and swore to become the King's man, and hold all his lands henceforward from him, and any other ransom that King Arthur might think good, and asked to depart free from Arthur's lands, together with his folk. And it was King Arthur's pleasure to accept this ransom. Of the King of Ireland I will speak no more.

The Wedding of Sir Agloval

Now King Arthur was so happy that he held a great court, that he might give whatever anyone might ask of him in largesse in reward. There came many to him, but none were of such renown or valiant as Sir Perceval and Sir Morien. The reward King Arthur gave them was exceedingly great. Sir Gawain told the king the entire story of Sir Morien, and of the matter between Sir Morien and his father, and the chance that had parted them. And being told in front of all the folk, everyone gazed upon Sir Morien in admiration.

With King Arthur's lands again at peace, Sir Morien thought he would make his father be wedded to his mother, and prayed his uncle to journey with him if he would. And Sir Perceval was right willing to do so. Further, said Sir Gawain and Sir Lancelot, they would also ride with Sir Morien, for his honor and good fellowship. And for this Sir Morien thanked them very much.

Thus they departed and went their way to the hermitage in Ireland. The conversation on their ride was happy, and they told many stories of things that had happened here and elsewhere, until they came to the seashore where without incident they took ship and crossed over, and rode straightaway to the hermitage of Perceval's uncle.

They were received with goodwill, and by now Sir Agloval was whole. Sir Morien asked him now that he was rightly healed if he would keep the oath he had sworn unto his mother? Sir Agloval answered he was whole, and sound and ready, "as God as my witness, I am altogether ready to do this!"

Perceval then asked "then why would we delay? Your son is so good a knight, so stout a warrior, that you ought to be proud he is your wife's son. Make yourself ready straight away and we will go with you. Sir Gawain and Sir Lancelot came here in good faith and good fellowship and would journey with us to the Moorish lands."

Then there was no longer delaying, but they made ready for the journey, and went on their way with Sir Morien, who knew the road better than any of them.

When at last they arrived, and the Moors had heard Sir Morien had brought his father with him, they assembled themselves together. Some of those assembled were excited to welcome Sir Morien home. But some were in favor of fighting to keep Sir Morien's father out of the kingdom, since they wanted to keep the inheritance they took from Sir Morien's mother, and especially to deny her her rightful place as their Queen. And partially to prevent the fair Sir Agloval from becoming their King, for they feared for their heritage. But when Sir Morien heard this, he grew so angry that he drew his sword and rode among them, slaying 15 of the nobles who were wanting to deny him his inheritance.

When those who had wanted to deny Sir Morien his inheritance saw this, they besought his grace and yielded to him his inheritance, giving it into the hand of his mother. And furthermore, to make up for their deceit, became her men and held their lands henceforth with her as their Queen. When this was done, they proclaimed her Queen over all the kingdom of the Moors.

Now they held a great bridal feast, and Sir Agloval and the Queen were wedded to each other. There was bliss and great rejoicing for 14 days, and even until nightfall they feasted with open doors. No one was denied anything on earth that they might desire! There was great merriment, many rich gifts were given, good horses, beautiful clothes, many shillings, many pounds, great plenty of all things by which men may more blithely live. Minstrels and heralds too received great largesses, for there was gold enough for them as well.

Sir Lancelot and Sir Gawain gladly abode there until the feast was ended, to honor the bride and groom.

What more shall I say? When the feast was ended and all the nobles departed, and all had taken leave, then it was in the mind of Sir Gawain, Sir Lancelot and Sir Perceval to return to King Arthur's court. For it was near to Pentecost, and the King would customarily hold high court. And this year, to celebrate his freedom, he was to hold a greater court than ever before, and also to honor Sir Galahed, Sir Lancelot's son, who would receive his knighthood that year on that holy day.

Sir Galahed, of course, would achieve the quest of the Grail, but that is part of another story. So here I will leave this tale and only say more how glad and happy King Arthur was to hear of the joy of Sir Morien's father and mother, and the valiant deeds Sir Morien had done in his own lands.

Now do I pray to God in words straightly, that he has mercy upon me when my life shall come to an end, and bring my soul to His heavenly kingdom. May he grant this, my prayer! Amen.

Further Reading

1. Alston. Challenging the whiteness of classics – remembering the Black Romans. The Conversation, February 3, 2022
2. Black Presence in Britain
   https://blackpresence.co.uk/about/faq/
3. Bowersox, Managing Editor. Black Central European Studies Network, available online at https://blackcentraleurope.com/
4. Eveleth. Not All the Knights of the Round Table Were White. Smithsonian Magazine, January 16, 2014
5. Isaac. The Invention of Racism in Classical Antiquity
6. Kennedy, et al. Race and Ethnicity in the Classical World: An Anthology of Primary Sources
7. Lomas, et al. Creating Ethnicities and Identities in the Roman World. Bulletin of the Institute of Classical Studies. Supplement (120): 1-10.
8. Medieval People of Color. https://medievalpoc.tumblr.com/
9. Museum Of London. Black Londoners Through Time. Also available online at:
   https://www.museumoflondon.org.uk/families/black-londoners-through-time/african-romans
10. Redfern, et al. Going south of the river: a multidisciplinary analysis of ancestry, mobility and diet in a population from

Roman Southwark, London. Journal of Archaeological Science, 2016.

11. Redfern, et al. "Written in Bone": New discoveries about the Lives and Burials of Four Roman Londoners. Britannia, 2017

12. Schierup. Genomic Ancestry of North Africans Supports Back-to-Africa Migrations. PLOS Genetics, 8 (1) (2012).

13. Snowden. Art and the somatic norm image. In: Before Color Prejudice, Harvard University Press.

14. Snowden. Blacks in Antiquity: Ethiopians in the Greco-Roman Experience

15. Weston (translator). Morien: A Metrical Romance Rendered into English Prose from the Mediaeval Dutch, 1901. Also available online at:

https://d.lib.rochester.edu/camelot/text/weston-morien

"Remembrance of the past may give rise to dangerous insights, and the established society seems to be apprehensive of the subversive contents of memory." - Herbert Marcuse